Love

and

Lemonade

Jamieson Wolf

Renaissance.
Diverse.Canadian Voices

LOVE AND LEMONADE ©2019 by Jamieson Wolf. All rights reserved. No part of this book may be used or reproduced in any manner whatsoever without written permission except in the case of brief quotations in critical articles and reviews. For more information, contact Renaissance Press. First edition.

Cover art, typesetting and interior design by.Nathan Fréchette. Edited by Evan McKinley and Nathan Fréchette.

Legal deposit, Library and Archives Canada, October 2019.

Paperback ISBN: 978-1-987963-64-9

Ebook ISBN: 978-1-987963-65-6

Renaissance Press

pressesrenaissancepress.ca

For Michael,
You have given me the world
and re-written my life.
I can't wait to write the next chapter with you.

Chapter One

"I can explain," Curtis said.

Devon stood there holding the flowers he had meant to leave for Curtis' birthday. They were supposed to be a surprise, but Devon was the one who was in shock. Curtis stood there looking like someone else entirely, like another person. Devon shook his head, closed his eyes and said a little internal prayer. Then he opened them again.

Curtis—if it was indeed him—was wearing a tight floor length ball gown in a brilliant pink colour. He had a blond wig on that matched his natural hair colour and it was done up in a large updo. A tiara blinked from atop his head. He was holding a purse that sparkled with iridescent rhinestones and his feet were clad in high heeled shoes in white leather that were covered in more rhinestones. He had makeup on and his eyelids that were marked in sparkling pink powder and his eyelashes were long and voluminous. He had another sparkly stone on his left cheek that looked like a beauty mark made of diamonds.

In short, Curtis sparkled.

Curtis looked shocked to see Devon. He actually jumped a little. "Hey handsome. I didn't expect you until later this evening. What are you doing here?"

Devon tried to play it cool. "What, a man can't bring his woman flowers for her birthday?"

Curtis let out a laugh and the sound calmed Devon a bit. "Oh, you silly man. I'm still a guy underneath this get up."

"You don't look like one now. How did you get boobs?"

"Believe it or not, plastic bags and hair gel. They make the most realistic breasts. A lot of drag queens use sand and balloons, but I find those too firm."

"Oh," Devon said.

The silence between them stretched on for too long. Devon looked at Curtis and still saw the man he loved, the man he adored, only he was wearing a dress.

After a few moments of silence, Curtis spoke again. "I'm sorry. I'm sorry you found out this way."

Shrugging, Devon said, "I just wanted to celebrate your birthday. I had all of these things planned, surprises and stuff I wanted to do for you."

"We can still do them! What did you have in mind?"

Instead of answering Curtis's question, Devon asked, "How long have you been doing this?"

"For a while now. A few years."

There was more silence while Devon tried to find a response. Finally, he spoke. "A few years?"

"Sure, my drag name is Carlotta Men. You may have seen me dressed up and performing in a few of the bars."

Love and Lemonade

The name did ring a bell. "You did that number where you sang 'These Boots Were Made for Walking' and actually walked on men's backs."

"Oh, you saw that one! I was really happy with that. Don't worry, all steps were strategically placed. No one actually got hurt."

"Glad to hear it," Devon said.

More silence filled the room. Curtis spoke again: "Look, Devon, I'm sorry you had to find out this way."

"I'm sorry, too."

"Are you mad because I'm a drag queen?"

Devon tried to keep the hurt out of his voice. "I'm mad because you didn't tell me."

He set the flowers down on the hallway table. "Happy birthday, Curtis."

Stepping out into the hallway, Devon closed the door. He placed his hand upon the wood and imagined Curtis doing the same.

He was about to turn away when he heard the click of high heels on hardwood. The door was thrown open and Curtis was standing there, looking like a woman.

"Would you at least come to my birthday drag show? I am preforming a number I'm dedicating to you."

Devon looked at this creature, this woman, and smiled. "Just try to stop me," he said. And then he walked away from Curtis, leaving his heart behind.

Chapter Two

"So, which one of you bitches is paying for this round? And it better not be me," Blaine said.

They had stopped going to The Cabin; they were seated around a table at a new bar that had opened called simply Centretown. It was upscale chic and Blaine didn't want to think of what the drinks would cost.

"You know what they say," Chuck said. "Once a beer whore…"

"Don't finish that sentence," Blaine said, giving Chuck a mock serious look. "Seriously, I can't be buying us all rounds all the time. I don't make much as a call centre agent, you know."

"Well, then, why fight fate? If you're fated to pay for our booze, the least you can do is stop bitching about it an accept it," Chuck said.

Blaine turned to Sebastian. "This is your fault. He never used to read before you. The most he would have said before is 'Shut up and pay beer, whore'. Now I get an argument about fate?"

Chuckling, Sebastian pulled Chuck closer to him and kissed him on the head. "I can't help it. He looks so sexy in his glasses. He looks like a naughty librarian. Books just complete the look."

"Honey, I didn't even know you could read," Nancy said.

"I can too read!" Chuck spat at him.

"Chucky cheese, all I ever saw you reading was Playgirl magazine. You know, the stuff with a lot of pictures."

"I don't need those kind of books now dumbass, not now that I have my Sebastian."

"So, what are you reading?" Justin asked. "Dick and Jane? See Spot Run? The Pokey Little Puppy?"

"That one always sounded like a book about Twinkies, to me," Mike said.

Nancy turned to look at them all. "Isn't he just the cutest?" He patted Mike's cheek and Mike smiled, blushing a little.

"So, are none of you going to help pay this round?" Blaine asked.

"I got you, Babe," Justin said taking out his wallet.

"My knight in shining armour," Blaine said.

"More like the knight of shining Amex, but I digress," Nancy said.

"Speaking of reading," Poppy said, pulling a cherry out of her cosmo. "What's the haps with the book tour? You haven't said anything in a few weeks."

"They're hammering out the details," Mike said. "He should know any day now."

"Actually…" Nancy looked sheepish. "They've already been nailed out. I'm leaving in week for a two-month, twelve city tour."

The smile that Mike had been wearing faltered and fell. "Oh."

Nancy took Mike's free hand in his. "Babe, don't be upset, it won't be too bad…"

Mike almost pouted. "I hate it when you go away. I get all mopey and don't know what to do with myself. That's just for a night or two when you're on the road to see clients. How do you think I'm going to handle a two month tour? I'll be a fucking wreck."

"Well…you could come with me? Nancy said, quietly.

Shock passed over Mike's face. "What? Do you mean it? Do you really honestly truly mean it?" The hope on his face lit up the room.

"Now, would I make up a story like that? I am a writer, but I'm not a liar. Of course I mean it. Melissa wouldn't hear of tearing us apart, so we arranged for an extra ticket."

A tear slid down Mike's cheek. "That's amazing! I love you so much."

Nancy said, "Not as much as I love you."

"Dear gods," Poppy said, laughing. "You guys are going to make me puke up my first cosmo!"

Chapter Three

William went out on the town.

The truth was, he didn't know what to do with himself. With David finally gone, he had a lot more time to himself now. He was no longer cowering in fear most of the time. He had stayed with Cordelia for a while, but then eventually moved back to his empty apartment.

It seemed so cavernous without Mike, without someone there to come home to. It had been months since David and the air smelled like fallen leaves and earth. It was a scent that calmed him. It made him think of the coming winter and of the ground covered in snow. He loved winter where everything looked so white and pure.

The snow also covered a multitude of sins.

Shaking his head, William kept walking. He was becoming mundane and depressed with spending so much time by himself. He hadn't dated anyone since David, if you could call the relationship he had with David dating.

Shivering, he pulled his leather coat tighter. He stopped walking and looked at The Cabin. He hadn't been there in so long, but the place hadn't changed. It still looked the same. William supposed that bars, unlike people, remained timeless.

William gave his head a shake. Hadn't he come out tonight so that he could be surrounded by people? Didn't he venture out into the night so that he could be amongst others? He wouldn't accomplish that standing here but, dear God, he wanted a cigarette. He would buy a pack on the way home, he decided.

Taking a deep breath, William walked inside.

The Cabin looked the same on the inside. The wooden ceiling beams were hung with lights and the walls were covered in wooden paneling. The same red velour couches were still there but there was a couch in the corner that was new. A couple sat on it making out.

He motioned to the bartender for a beer and then sat on one of the barstools. He closed his eyes and let himself move to the music. William had missed the music, how it could sink into your body and compel you to dance, how it moved you and how you moved with it. He would need a few more before he got up onto the dance floor.

The bartender placed a beer in front of him and a shot of Jägermeister. William looked at it. "I didn't order this."

The bartender, a guy called Sean, smiled at him. "You've only been here for a few minutes and you've already turned someone's crank. That guy over there bought your beer and the shot."

Sean pointed to the corner of The Cabin and he saw a man with gorgeous red hair raise his own drink in salute. He was seated at a table instead of one of the barstools. "If you don't want him, let me know, I love gingers." He gave William a devilish grin.

"You leave him to me. And pour me another shot of Jägermeister, will you?"

Taking his beer in one hand and the two shots in the other, he made his way to the corner table. "Hey there."

The guy smiled. "Hi."

"Thanks for the drinks. You didn't have to do that."

"Sure, I did. You were sitting there looking all lonely. The least I could do was brighten up your night."

The man had gorgeous green eyes that shone like emeralds lit by the moon. William actually felt a little swoon coming on. "My name's William."

"That's funny. You don't look like a William. I think I'll call you Will."

"Okay, since we're on the subject of names, what's yours?"

"My name is Zack. Nice to meet you Will." He held up the shot of Jägermeister that William had gotten for him. "Cheers."

He smiled and William nearly came in his pants. Zack had a gorgeous dimple that graced one cheek when he smiled. He clinked his shot glass against Zack's and threw the Jägermeister back.

"Thanks, Zack. That was nice."

"Thank you, too. You didn't have to buy me anything."

"It's all good man." The DJ started spinning another song that was heavy on the base. The music called to William to get up on that dance floor and let himself go. "You want to finish our drinks and go dance our asses off?"

"I'd love to, but I can't dance."

"Sure you can, everyone can dance. I look like I'm having a full body dry heave standing up when I dance, but I still do it." William gave Zack a wicked grin.

"No, you don't understand, I really can't dance. I would love to, but I can't."

William saw storms within Zack's eyes and there was a grim set to Zack's lips from things he didn't want to say. Mike had gotten like that when they were together, and Mike was being careful with his words.

"Hey, it doesn't matter we can dance some other time." William reached out and took hold of Zack's hand. He knew it would be warm, but what William didn't expect was the electric charge that ran up his arm. He looked into Zack's eyes and saw that he had felt the spark, too.

"This is nice." Zack said. "Besides, I'd like to at least get to know you a bit before I take you to bed. Tell me, are you a top or a bottom?"

William was taking a sip of his beer and nearly choked on a mouthful. "Wow, you cut to the chase, don't you?" He felt a blush redden his skin. "That is, I mean, I did, I do want to, but I haven't-"

Zack squeezed his hand and William felt another rush of warmth up his arm. "It's all good. We can just get to know each other if you want."

10

William smiled. "That would be nice." He took a sip of his beer.

"But I wouldn't say no to a hot make out session. Plus, I want to see if your dick looks as good out of the jeans as it does in them."

William spit out a mouthful of beer.

Chapter Four

Romilda wondered when her life had become perfect.

Or, she amended, pretty damn close to perfect as there was no such thing as perfection nowadays anyway.

She turned and looked at Gaston, at his proud forehead and his hair that had gotten all mused up during the night. His breathing was soft and even and she watched his chest rise and fall with each breath. It was amazing how much calmness Gaston brought to her life when it had been so frantic before.

His deep breathing lessened, and she watched as his eyes fluttered open. Looking at her, Gaston smiled. "Why is it that I always wake up to you watching me sleep?"

"It's one of my favourite things to do."

"Honey, you need to find a new hobby. I'm not that exciting."

"Oh, I think you are. You make me feel better than I've ever felt in my whole life. I want to spend the rest of it watching and loving you."

He took her hand in his and kissed the back of it. "I love you, Romy."

"I love you too, Gaston."

She lay back down and snuggled closer to him, basking in his warmth. It was still dark out and she could see the stars through her window. She felt so content, it was frightening to think that only a few months ago, she thought she would be alone forever.

"So, I've been thinking," Gaston said.

"A dangerous thing to do."

"Indeed, but sometimes, this old brain of mine can't help it."

"So, what were you thinking?"

"Well, I think it's time that you met my daughter."

"You have children?"

"Just the one. A beautiful daughter named Isabella. My wife and I tried for more, but we were only blessed with Isabella."

"I don't know, Gaston. Can't it just be the two of us for now?"

"Hey, now. I've met your family, your son and ex-wife and all of your friends. I have very few friends and only one daughter. Since I'm going to spend the rest of my life with you, it's only fair that she meets you."

"Oh, I don't know…"

Gaston propped himself up on his elbows and looked at her. "What's with the hesitation?"

"Well…what if she doesn't like me?"

"What's not to like?"

"What I mean is…what if she doesn't like the fact that I'm trans?"

There was a beat of silence after she said this. Finally, Gaston spoke. "That shouldn't matter. When I look you, all I see is my beautiful and gorgeous Romy. You're all woman, inside and out. You can't be afraid of what other people think of you, only what you think of yourself. Besides, I think you're gorgeous and it's really my opinion that matters, right?"

Romilda let out a laugh that sounded like music. "I guess so."

"Ain't no guessing about it, honey. Now come here and snuggle close. We got an early shift at the library."

"Don't you mean that I have an early shift at the library?"

"Honey, where you go, I go. Now come on. You may not need it, but I need my beauty sleep."

Chapter Five

When Poppy got home, she found Dava cleaning the house. Again.

Dava had been cleaning a lot lately. She had always been a neat person and they kept a clean home, but Dava was taking cleanliness to the next level. She mopped the floors before work, and when she came home, she was forever wiping down every surface.

Poppy had tried to get Dava to talk about what was bothering her, but Dava kept saying that she was okay, that she was all right, that she was fine, never better. Poppy knew that something was wrong, she knew it in her gut.

Right now, Dava was cleaning the kitchen counters with bleach. The smell of it was strong enough to make Poppy's eyes water. Carefully, so as not to startle her, Poppy wrapped her arms around her from behind and pulled her close.

"Hey Babe," Dava said. "I'm almost done."

"From the smell, I think you've done the counters a few times."

Dava let out a huff of breath. "I've only cleaned them twice, I need to clean them three times so that they are totally clean."

"Honey, honey, come here." She turned Dava around and pulled her as close as she could. "You don't have to clean the counters three times, vacuum the carpets five times, or do the windows eight times. You don't have to. What you do have to do is tell me what's wrong."

Dava stilled as if terrified. "Nothing's wrong, everything's fine, everything is okay."

She didn't look okay. There was worry etched on her face in every line. Dava hadn't been sleeping well for weeks now. She had been tossing and turning at night, mumbling in her sleep. Poppy knew that she wasn't resting, wasn't sleeping.

"Honey," Poppy said. "Tell me what's wrong. Please."

It was the please that did it. Dava dissolved into tears and, for a while, all Poppy could do was hold her close, murmuring soft words to her. Finally, Dava pulled back, her face streaked with tears. It looked as if her face had pieces of crystal etched into it.

Dava looked at Poppy with large eyes filled with fear. "I'm just so afraid, all the time. I'm afraid that Fred will come back for us, that he will find us."

"He went to prison honey. For a very long time. He won't be getting out any time soon."

"Yeah, but what about your baby? Because of me, you lost your child. You lost your baby."

The mention of her miscarriage, her baby, hurt Poppy, but only for a millisecond. She couldn't dwell on that now. She had to take care of Dava.

16

"Honey, we talked about this already. Come here."

Poppy took hold of Dava's hand and led her over to the couch. She sat Dava down and wiped at her face with a tissue. Poppy's heart ached for her lover. "I don't know what to do for you, Dava." She said. "Tell me what to do, what I can do to make it better."

"I'm just so afraid all the time now. I know we're fine, that we're okay and we have that to be thankful for, but every time the doorbell rings or there's a knock on the door, I think it's him."

"Do you want to move? Maybe we could find another apartment?"

"No, it wouldn't matter where we lived. I just feel like I've lost control of my life. I don't know what to do. I'm sorry I'm like this. I just figure if I can control *something*, I'll be okay."

"You will be okay. Look, let's go talk to Blaine tomorrow, okay? He'll have an idea, I'm sure. In the meantime, how about I draw you a bath?"

Dava's face brightened. "What will you do while I'm having a bath?"

"Oh honey, I'll be in the bath with you. Let's see what trouble we can get up to, shall we?"

Chapter Six

Cordellia sat looking through her notebooks, sipping a glass of pink lemonade and vodka. *Hey, why mess with a classic?* she thought.

"So I talked to Mr. Stevens and we can have the hall for practically nothing! I was out the other day with Romilda and found my wedding dress. Oh, wait until you see it, I look raving in it! I'm still not sure that I'm going to get it, but it's so beautiful. I'll bring Blaine with me to get his input. I've also talked to Talia the other day at her restaurant and she's agreed to do the catering for us at her family rate."

Joe looked at her with a large grin on his face. "What's the family rate?"

"Well, free, as long as she's invited to the wedding."

"She can't expect us to let her cater our wedding and not charge us anything."

"That's what I said. She wouldn't hear of it. I argued with her and she said that she would take an invite to the wedding, a larger piece of cake than everyone else and that we pay for her dress."

Joe let out a loud laugh that ended with a few coughs. He banged his fist and there were tears sliding down his cheeks. "That's one heck of a deal!"

"Don't be silly! I told her that we would certainly not go for that and would pay her the proper rate."

"How'd she take that?"

"She grumbled a lot about her family being stubborn and then gave me more coffee. So, I guess everything is okay."

"It's more than okay, isn't it? We're finally getting married." He went to Cordellia and put his arms around her. "I don't want to wait another moment. I can't believe that we've had to wait so long."

Her mouth grimaced in pain. "I'm sorry, Joe. You have no idea how sorry I am that I ran away from you."

Taking her hands, Joe looked Cordellia in the eyes. "I have told you again and again that that was old business, water under the bridge. Why are you so intent to focus on what was instead of what we have now?"

"Because I'm kicking myself. We could have had almost thirty more years together."

"Honey, it doesn't matter. None of that does, as long as we have right now together."

"Well, now and the rest of our lives." Cordellia smiled and kissed him softly, not seeing the look of panic that flashed across his face.

When she pulled away, the look was gone. "Yes, yes of course. What do you have left in that remarkable book of yours?" Joe asked her.

"Well, dress, check. Catering, check. Hall, check. I guess all that's left to do is decide on a date and invite everyone. I was thinking a spring wedding, all that new growth. Won't it be lovely to be getting married when the tulips and flowers are out?"

"I was actually thinking something a little sooner than the spring."

"Oh, anxious for the wedding night?" Cordellia joked. "How soon were you thinking?"

"I was thinking about sometime next week," he said.

Cordellia was taken aback. "Honey, don't you think that's rushing it a little?"

He took her hands again. "I've spent my entire life waiting for you. I don't want to wait another moment. I want to make you the happiest that you've ever been. Won't you let me do that?"

Warmth spread though Cordellia and she kissed him again. "Of course," she said. "Well, this calls for a glass of wine! I'll get the glasses and you get the bottle of red, okay?" She gave his butt a quick pat as she went towards the kitchen.

Joe ran his hand through his hair and wondered if he could go through with this.

Chapter Seven

Dillon wondered if it was possible to die from having an erection.

"Rebecca, you're killing me here."

She let out a giggle and gave him a big smile. "Gosh, men are funny."

"Look, when you asked if I could come over while you modeled clothes for me, I was all for it. Who doesn't love to look at the woman they love model clothes she looks hot in?"

"You still haven't mentioned the problem." Rebecca said.

"You failed to tell me that you were going to model lingerie."

She put a finger to her lips. "Really? I was sure I'd mentioned that."

"Nope." Dillon let out a grunt while he adjusted himself. "You didn't."

"Hmmm…" Rebecca's smile widened. "I still fail to see how this is a problem. Most men would be very happy to have their girlfriend model lingerie for them."

"I'm sure. But they would be hoping that it would lead to something."

She came closer to him and rubbed a hand along his cheek. "Who says that this won't?"

"Oh, you mean it will?" Dillon looked up at the woman he loved. She was wearing a black lace bra and panties that left little if anything to the imagination, but still managed to leave a few scraps of skin hidden. How could women show so much skin, yet still remain so covered? He would never understand it.

"Of course it will, silly. Would I go through this much effort and not give you a treat for being a good boy?"

Dillon let out a long, slow breath. "I don't know, that depends on how sadistic you were planning on being."

Letting out a laugh that was like fingers along his skin, Rebecca leaned down closer to him. "Not very...unless you want me to be really naughty."

Dillon tried to keep his gaze on her eyes but he couldn't help it. I mean, they were *right* there.

"We can play in a moment, hot stuff. But first...I have a favour to ask you."

"Anything." He said. "Anything you want, you can have it. "

"I want to have Devon over for dinner."

"Anything but that."

Rebecca stood and crossed her arms in front of her chest. "And why not?"

"Honey, you know how I feel about my brother."

"Yes, I know what he did to your family and to your mom. Dillon, it was her choice to give him the money. You know that right?"

"Yeah, but he didn't have to ask her."

"He was an addict and a sex worker. I'd say that was rock bottom, don't you?"

He sat back and threw his hands up in the air. "I don't know why you're always standing up for him."

"Because he's my best friend! Since we moved in together, I've always gone out to see him. Did you know he's seeing someone now? A really nice guy named Curtis."

"He must have low standards in men."

She smacked his arm. "Curtis is actually a very lovely man. And you, sir, are being an asshole."

Dillon snorted.

"You have to let go of the hate, babe. It'll age you before your time. And drive a wedge in between us." She uncrossed her arms. "I love you, Dillon, but I also love Devon. Not in the way I love you, but he was all I had for a long time. Please don't make me choose between my best friend and the man I love."

He was quiet for a few minutes. Then he spoke. "Dinner. One drink, no appetizers or dessert, but he can stay for a cup of coffee afterwards or tea or whatever."

A wide smile broke out on Rebecca's face. "Thanks babe."

"You know I only agreed because you look like a goddess in that lingerie?"

"I know. Why do you think I wore them?"

She leaned down and kissed him and he forgot to be angry with her.

Chapter Eight

Victoria took in Blaine's latest work with a shrewd eye and pursed lips. She walked around the easel to observe the canvass from different angles and even got close enough to the canvass to probably get high of the fumes from the paint.

"What's she the doing?" Justin whispered. "It looks like she's going to make out with your new portrait. I never knew that my mother was a lesbian."

Blaine let out a snort that he managed to turn into a cough. He had done a portrait of Mo Collins. After the ordeal with David and William, they had struck up a friendship with the woman that Blaine had helped with a few of her more technological problems at the call centre.

Far from being nervous about meeting her in person, Blaine felt as if he was meeting an old friend. They got along like a house on fire. Justin was pulled into the mix and soon, it was as if Justin, too, had known Mo all his life.

Blaine had asked her if he could paint her at their last get together. Mo had invited them over for a home cooked meal. She had blushed at the idea of being painted.

"Oh, but you don't want to go painting an old broad like me."

"And why not? There is nothing old about you," Blaine said.

"I'm seventy-five years old. No one would want to look at a painting of me. They'd be able to see every wrinkle."

Blaine reached out and clasped her hand in one of his. "Every line tells a story of the life that you've lived, the path that you've been on to get where you've gotten today."

She raised an eyebrow and was silent for a moment before erupting into an ear-splitting guffaw. Mo wagged a finger at Justin. "Oh, you keep an eye on this one. He'll charm the pants right off of you with the way he speaks."

"He already has," Justin said, smiling.

Mo let out another loud snort and then nodded her head. "All right, all right, I'll do it. Now, I don't have to get naked, do I? I have horrible stretch marks. My abdomen looks like a map of the London underground."

Blaine laughed. "No, no, I don't paint you naked. I just need a photo of you as you are now. One that you like. I'll paint you from that."

"Well, that sounds like a lot less fun, but okay." She took Blaine's hand in hers and squeezed it. "I'm so glad that we finally met. A voice on the phone is no substitute for the real thing."

"That's so true. If you want, I can paint you here and we can get to know each other. I know you have a granddaughter, but that's pretty much all I know."

25

Mo gave Blaine a quick hug. "That's so sweet. You'd do that for a little old lady like me?"

"Sure I would."

Over the next few weeks, Blaine visited Mo Seagrave at her home and painted her. Blaine worked from the photo but mostly from looking at her as she talked about her family and her granddaughter. He had wanted to capture the laugh lines on her faced as she laughed with abandon. He wanted to capture the essence of her.

Blaine was surprised by how much he liked Mo. He came to think of her as his aunt or grandmother. Most of all, though, he thought of her as his friend.

When he had finished the portrait, he showed Mo, while holding his breath. It was always like this when he showed someone his interpretation of them. She regarded the painting with something approaching shock. She said nothing for a few minutes. Blaine began to worry that he'd done her a disservice when her face had finally broken out into a huge smile.

Approaching the painting, she held out her hand towards it, to run along her own face. She stopped short of touching the painting but when Mo turned to face him, there were tears sliding down her cheeks. "Is this how you see me?" she asked.

Blaine shook his head. "This is how you look." He motioned at the canvass. "This is how the world sees you."

Love and Lemonade

A tear slid down Mo's cheek and she wiped it away. She took a moment to pat her grey hair that was elegantly coiffed. "Damn I look hot! I look pretty damn good for seventy-five, don't I, boys?"

"That you do Ms. Seagrave," Justin said.

Mo gave Justin a hard look. "Now don't make me give you the same talk I gave to this one about calling me Ms. anything. You are family. Family doesn't use such stuffy things like Mr. and Mrs., now, do they?"

Justin grinned. "I suppose they don't."

Blaine had told her that he wanted the painting to be in his upcoming exhibition and she was all atwitter. "Oh, that's so fancy! Can I come? Do models usually attend exhibitions featuring them?"

"Of course. It would be an honour to have you there."

He gave her a big hug, trying to communicate his thanks in the embrace. Mo squeezed him back as if she understood.

Blaine had promised to take care of the portrait and that it was hers. He would bring it back to her after the exhibition. When she tried to pay him for it, he waved the money away. "I didn't do this for money. I did this for you."

Her eyes were glassy again and she smiled a watery smile. "You truly are an angel, Blaine. Thank you."

Chapter Nine

Victoria stepped away from Mo's canvas, her eyes filled with a bright light that could mean only one thing: She was happy with the canvas.

Victoria had been true to her word. She had gotten in touch with a friend of hers, Remmington Pecora, a woman that ran her own gallery and knew all the artists in the City. She had called Blaine up one morning and promptly invited herself over for tea.

"When Vicky said that you were a talent that rivaled Klimt for the power he created with his eyes, I had to come immediately. Now I see what she meant." She stood looking at canvases that were sitting on a circle of easels that Blaine had arranged around the living room. Remmington walked around and then stopped at the portrait of Mo. "This is extraordinary. They all are."

She walked over to him. "Blaine, do you have any more canvases?"

"Yeah, I have lots."

"Define lots." Remmington said with a smile. She had pert lips and an oval face, green eyes and blond hair that was in an elegant updo.

"Well, I have these here and then another forty or fifty of them that are in storage. I have lots that I've given for presents, probably about thirty of them."

Her smile widened. She pointed at a piece he had done of Poppy. "You know this woman." It wasn't a question. "Do you know all of these people?"

"Not all of them, no. Sometimes, it's just a random person that I see in my day to day life. Their face sticks with me until I get it out on the canvass."

"Well, you bring them all to life. I'm very impressed."

Blaine was a little nervous now so he thought he should just ask, get it out and whatever happens would happen. "Ms. Pecora,"

"Remmy, please."

"Remmy, then. Victoria mentioned that you might be able to hang a few of my paintings in your gallery. Do you think you will be able to?"

"No, I don't think that will do at all." Blaine was crestfallen until she spoke again. "I think your work merits its own exhibition, don't you?"

From that moment, his whole world had seemed to change. She was calling him things like distinguished and revolutionary, she called him an *artist*. Blaine had always called himself that, but to have a woman who ran a gallery call him that was beyond his wildest dreams.

Justin had been elated when Blaine had told him. "Your own exhibition? That's fantastic!"

"I know! She was talking about thirty canvasses plus art cards for starters and possibly prints of others that aren't for sale." He hugged Justin closer. "I'm an artist!"

"I've always known you were from the moment I saw your first painting."

Blaine kissed him. "I know. Thank you."

"For what?"

"Just for being you."

When Victoria had gotten home, she had been full of smiles. "Remy tells me that she loves your stuff. Your own gallery exhibition, Blaine! How exciting!" She gave him a small kiss on the cheek. "Now you better get working, shouldn't you? You only have a month to get all of your work ready."

That had been three weeks ago. He had gathered all of the pieces he loved the most, but he wanted a central piece to the exhibition. That was Mo's piece. There was just something about it. There was a light contained within it, as if he had captured part of her spirit as well as per physical attributes.

Victoria took Blaine's hands in hers. "This is truly a lovely piece, Blaine. When you said you were going to do a portrait of some old lady you had never met, I thought it was just the eccentric behaviour of an artist, like wearing plaid with stripes and no underwear, or wool socks with sandals in the middle of summer!" She threw back her head and let out a tinkling laugh.

Love and Lemonade

Blaine and Justin had taught themselves to keep smiling, no matter what Victoria had sometimes said. Justin knew that his mother had come a long way, but she still had a hell of a long way to go.

Chapter Ten

Curtis picked at his eggs and wondered how his life had gone to shit so quickly.

"Honey, you have to eat something. Your eggs are starting to look like street walkers at night, all mashed up with nowhere to go. What's wrong?" Sasha said, patting his hand.

"I messed everything up. Everything."

"Curtis, sweetie, it's not that bad. Surely it's not."

"I didn't tell Devon about being a drag queen and he came over this morning to surprise me for my birthday when I was trying on my outfit for tonight."

"Oh," Sasha said. She took a sip of her coffee before responding. "I could see how that would put a wrench in things. How did he react?"

"He was a total gentleman about it. He was shocked and was upset that I had never told him anything about it but agreed to come to my birthday show."

"Honey, that's so sweet!"

"I know!" Curtis moaned.

"If it's so perfect, why are you acting like it's the end of the world?"

"Well, the fact that I wasn't honest with him makes me wonder. I mean, how much do I love him if I didn't tell him?"

"I don't know. Why didn't you tell him? You're a fabulous drag queen. You can move across the stage with ease that most women don't have. I walk like a trucker for fuck sake and so do most drag queens."

"I know." He sighed again. "I just couldn't stand him walking away from me, you know? I hate that look that I get from guys when they hear I'm a drag queen. It's either a transvestite horn-dog who gets off on men who wear women's clothes, or they fall in love with the drag queen part of me and not the male part of me, you know?"

"I don't know. I have no idea why you even do it, as fabulous as you are when you're performing."

"That's just it, it's all a performance. It's about living outside of yourself, even just for a moment." He took a sip of coffee and was silent for a moment as he tried to put his thoughts in order. "I know what I like, I'm a man and I like men. There's no confusion there. I just want to embrace both sides of myself, the male and the female. Plus, you ladies get better clothes! Add to all that the confidence that I get from being able to get up on stage and parade around, lip synching to music! It's like a grown-up version of play acting. I get to be myself while living beyond myself."

"That's pretty deep. Most drag queens just say they love women's clothing," Sasha said.

"Well, that too. I do look fabulous in a push up and a pair of stilettos."

"It does make your legs look great," Sasha said, taking a bite of her omelette. "What are you going to do about Devon?" She put her hand on his again and gave it a squeeze. "Why does this all make you so sad if he's okay with Monica Diamond?"

Curtis looked at her with sparkles in his eyes. "Don't you see Sasha? He loves me no matter what size I am, even though I don't fit the mould for a typical gay man. He doesn't even mind that I'm a drag queen!" His smile brightened up his whole being. "I think I'm beginning to realize how much I love him!"

He took a sip of his coffee. "Plus, his cock is fucking huge!"

Sasha spit out her coffee.

Chapter Eleven

"Something is wrong with Cassandra." Sebastian said.

Chuck looked at her and shrugged. "I don't see a problem. She looks okay to me."

"She's been way more moody than usual lately and has been walking around with a chip on her shoulder."

"Babe, she's a nineteen-year-old woman. I would think something is wrong if she wasn't behaving like that."

"You don't know my daughter. She's sarcastic as hell, yes, but she's also a fun-loving person, full of light. Always making a joke, at someone's expense usually, true, but nonetheless. I think something's wrong."

"Well, I don't know nothing about children. Having been a child myself most of my life until I met you, I'm not the person to ask." He gave Sebastian a quick kiss.

"You don't think anything's wrong?" Sebastian rubbed at his forehead. "I know my daughter, and this isn't her."

"So why don't you ask her? If she's living with us now, we should know what's going on."

"Okay, Babe. Cassie!"

"What?!" Cassandra called from inside of her room.

"Can you come out here and talk to us?" Sebastian said.

"We're talking just fine now."

35

Sebastian sighed. "That may be, but I'd like to talk to you without a piece of wood between us. Care to join us in the living room? I'll pour us a glass of wine."

There was the sound of her door opening and she clomped into the living room. "I'll have a glass of red followed by another glass of something stronger."

"I will pour you a glass of wine if you tell me what's going on."

Cassandra gave him an appraising look. "Are you bribing me with wine?"

"So, what if I am?" Sebastian put his hands on his hips.

"So, nothing. I'm just stating the obvious. You should have bribed me with wine a long time ago." She took three glasses down from the cupboard. She pulled a bottle that was sitting on the counter towards her and poured a generous amount in a glass. Saying nothing, she threw that back and then poured more, this time in each glass.

"How's the wine?" Chuck asked, raising his eyebrows.

"It's good. It has tones of bitterness and anger but has a nice fucktard body," Cassie said sardonically.

Chuck tried to hold the laughter in, he really did, but it erupted out of him with the force of a fog horn. He laughed even louder when he saw Cassie and Sebastian's shocked faces and soon, they were laughing right along with him. The laughter reached a fever pitch before gently dying away to a comfortable silence that lasted until Cassie spoke.

"Well fuck me sideways, I needed that."

"I'm sorry for laughing." Chuck said.

"Don't be. I needed that and it makes everything seem not as dire as it was."

"What's the problem, sweetheart?" Sebastian asked.

"Oh, you know, just the normal every day broken heart." She sighed and took a sip of her wine.

Chapter Twelve

"You have great eyes," William said

Zack blushed. "I bet you say that to all the guys you're trying to pick up."

"Nah, just you. I haven't dated in a long time."

Zack nodded and took a sip of his beer. "Why? You're hot and I'm sure there are lots of guys out there that would date you."

William wondered how he would answer. "I had some shit I needed to sort out. I was pretty messed up."

Letting out a laugh, Zack clinked his glass against William's. "I hear that. I've been working on getting some shit together myself." He smiled. "I can't imagine you'd have a lot of shit to put right, though."

"Oh, you'd be surprised."

"Try me."

"We'll save that for another time, if you don't mind."

"Did you want there to be another time? I haven't even sucked your dick yet," Zack said with a mischievous grin.

William felt a nervous twinge of heat in his stomach. "Are you sure you don't want to dance? The beat is really good."

"Nah, can we go somewhere though? I want to get out of the bar and into the fresh air."

"Sure, if you'd like."

William stood and put his coat back on. He looked back at Zack to see him pulling out a cane from underneath his chair. He stood with it and William noticed Zack about to lose his balance.

Stepping forward, William balanced Zack by putting a hand on either shoulder. "Careful, you look like you were about to fall for a second there. How much did you have to drink anyway?"

With a hurt look on his face, he brushed William's hands off of him. "I'm not drunk."

"Sure you're not. Look it's okay if you can't hold your booze. Lord knows that I was a cheap date for a while."

"I'm not fucking drunk."

"There's no shame in it, even if you are."

"Look, can we just go?"

Zack sounded pissed. William followed quietly behind Zack and watched his hair as the light hit it. His hair looked as if it were made of the sun itself. It shone a bright red gold colour. God, he wanted to run his fingers through it.

They came to the front of the bar where there were steps leading down to the street. Zack looked at the steps as if they were the devil. There was no railing and there were only three steps to get down.

"Here, let me help you," William said.

"I don't need your help. I have to learn to do this on my own."

He took a step down to the first step, but then he over balanced and fell to the ground, rolling over the final two steps. Zack hit the ground and let out a loud cry.

William jumped down and pulled Zack up, clutching him close. "I've got you, you're okay." He looked at Zack to make sure he was all right. "I've got you, you're okay."

They looked at each other for a moment and then William kissed him. It was a long, slow kiss and the heat built up slowly but with increasing intensity. When William pulled away, he was breathing heavily.

"That was nice," William said.

"Yeah, it was. I'm sorry for falling. I'm kind of embarrassed."

"There's nothing to be embarrassed about. Everyone gets drunk from time to time." He ran a thumb along Zack's lips.

To William's surprise, a tear slid down Zack's cheek. "I'm not fucking drunk." He whispered. "This was a mistake; this whole evening was a mistake. I'm sorry."

Zack pulled back and made to walk away from him, but William held onto Zack's wrist. "Can't I get your number? I'll give you mine."

Nodding, Zack pulled out a piece of paper and jotted down his number. "Thank you for a lovely evening." Handing the paper to William, Zack went to walk away.

"Wait, I haven't given you my number yet."

"It's all good. You don't have to call me." There were tears sliding down Zack's face.

William took Zack's hand in his. "Please, I want to."

Zack quickly handed William his pen and another piece of paper and William wrote down his number and handed it to Zack.

"Is there anything I can do to help? Do you want me to walk you home?"

Zack shook his head and stepped away from William. "I'll get a cab. It's all good. You can go back in if you want, don't worry about me."

"Let me at least wait with you while you get your cab. I thought you wanted to have a hot make out session," William said.

Zack let out a wet laugh. "Yeah, who'd want to make out with me?"

"I do." William said. "Very much." He leaned forward and kissed Zack again, softly. "Tell me what's wrong. Maybe I can help?"

Zack looked at William and William saw how deep the green went. William saw sorrow in those eyes. "No one can help me," Zack said.

A cab pulled up and Zack stepped away again. "I had a lovely evening. Thanks, Will. You are a true gentleman."

Zack slid into the cab and William continued looking after it, long after it had driven away.

Chapter Thirteen

"What do you mean honey?" Sebastian asked. "Who broke your heart?"

"Just this guy I was sleeping with."

"You were sleeping with someone?" There was steel in his voice.

"Chill pops, we were careful. Thing about it is, I came here for him."

"I thought you came to live with me."

"Yeah, that too. But we met and hooked up online. It was going well, but…well, nothing. Nothing, it's nothing. Let's have more wine and I'm ordering some pizza."

Walking up to his daughter, Sebastian put an arm around her shoulders and pulled her close. "What happened honey? You know that you can talk to Chuck and I about anything, right? There's no topic off limits."

"Except llamas," Chuck said.

Sebastian gave him a dark look. "Llamas? Really?"

"Have you seen those things? They're creepy and they spit."

Cassandra let out a little laugh. "No, it's okay…" A tear slid down her cheek.

"Honey, this is obviously upsetting you. What is it?"

She was silent for a little bit and her silence stretched until it filled the kitchen with words left unsaid. Finally, she spoke. "Well, I guess it was you, Dad."

"Me, what do you mean? "

"Well, I told Geoff about you. We'd gotten really close so I thought I could tell him anything. I told him about my father and then…" Cassie's eyes scrunched up and when she opened them again, her eyes were filled with unshed tears. "I thought I could trust him with anything, so I told him all about how you used to be…about who you were to me now, and who you were when I was growing up." A deep red blush flooded her cheeks that clashed with her red hair. More tears slid down her cheeks. "I'm sorry, Dad."

The unshed tears broke free of their barrier and slid down her face. Sebastian gathered her to him and he hugged her close, trying to convey everything he could not say in that embrace. He didn't want to tell her that it wasn't her secret to share, that she should have left that up to him, if it even came up.

Instead, he left those words unsaid. She didn't need to hear that right now. Instead, he stroked her back like he used to when she was younger and had had a nightmare. "It'll be okay care bear."

She looked up at him with red rimmed eyes. "Really?"

"Really, really. You don't need an asshole like that in your life, someone who was unable to accept part of your family."

"Besides, he's probably a douchebag," Chuck said.

"I don't think we need to hear that kind of language," Sebastian said.

"Hey, she's nineteen, not nine. You got a name you want to call him sweetheart?"

"Fuckwit," Cassie said.

"That's good, give me another one."

"Asshole galaxy galore!"

"Oooh!" Chuck said. "I like that. It sounds almost glamourous! Give me one more honey!"

"Douchebag dumbass dinglefart!"

Then Cassie did the most wondrous thing: she laughed. Despite the tears streaming down her face, she laughed and the sound was like magic to Sebastian.

Sebastian watched as his daughter began to smile and he looked over at Chuck and was filled with so much love for both of them.

He also swore to himself that, if he ever ran into this Geoff boy, he would have to kick his ass.

Chapter Fourteen

Nancy tried not to let out a squeal of glee as the train started to move. He was going on tour!

He hadn't believed that it was going to happen until Melissa Molina had sent him the tickets or the itinerary. Then, as the day to travel got closer, he imagined that he would wake up at some point, that all of this was a dream that would cease to really be happening to him.

However, Nancy had to admit that this was happening. He sat in first class beside Mike, his book on his lap. He had kept the first copy that Melissa had given him as his own. He would be reading from it at events and promotional stops.

Melissa said that his book had climbed up to the number two spot on the New York Times. He rubbed his hand over the book cover and smiled to himself.

Beside him, Michael let out a little chuckle. "You look like the cat that got the cream."

Nancy took his hand and squeezed it. "Honey, I got you. I can have your cream any time I want." He gave Mike a wicked grin.

"That's not what I meant, and you know it. No, you just looked so happy right now."

"How can I not be? I have you in my life, I wrote a book that is doing well and I'm going on tour?"

Mike squeezed his hand again and kissed the back of Nancy's head. "I'm so happy that I'm with you."

"The feeling is mutual, Babe." His cell phone rang. "Hold on a second Babe, gotta see who this is."

Melissa Molina showed up on the call display. He answered right away. "Oh, hey girl! How's my favourite publisher?"

"I'm doing wonderfully. Just wanted to touch base to make sure that you got on the train."

"Yep, first stop Montreal, next stop Toronto and then onward into Canada and the US. We're almost in Montreal. Thanks for the first-class ticket, girl, you shouldn't have."

"Please, it's the least I could do. Your book is selling like hotcakes! We can't keep them stocked fast enough, so think of it as my way of saying thanks. Oh, and I booked you and Michael in the honeymoon suites in all your hotels. Indulge yourselves, Clarence, okay?"

Hearing his real name instead of his nickname had always been a bit jarring to Nancy, but he was starting to get used to it by now. Melissa always said that he didn't look like a Nancy. He always told her that it wasn't about how he *looked*, it was about how he *felt*.

"Okay," he told her. "I will do as you command."

"Oh, I almost forgot! We got a call from your mother at the office!"

Nancy felt his world fall out of balance a little bit. "My mother?"

"Yeah! She said that she read your book and wanted to see you. Why would she get in touch with me, Nancy? Wouldn't she just call you?"

He tried to make his voice sound normal, tried to make it sound as if nothing was wrong. "Oh, she probably lost my number again. She's always doing that, you know how mothers are."

"Yeah, mine still can't figure out how to use the DVD player. It's all good though. I gave her your itinerary and she will be meeting you in Montreal! She has the address of your hotel too, and the room number, so she knows where to find you."

"Oh," Nancy said. "That's lovely!" He injected some false happiness into his voice.

"I knew you'd be pleased! Good luck at your event tomorrow! I know you will do beautifully!"

She hung up and Nancy felt his stomach fall to the ground. Michael looked at him. "What's wrong?" He said, concerned. "You look like you've seen a ghost!"

Chapter Fifteen

Curtis tried to remind himself again, for the thousandth time, not to be nervous. He had nothing to be nervous about. Just because the man he loved would be out in the audience watching him perform, well that was nothing to be nervous about. Just because Devon made Curtis' heart melt and Curtis still felt bad for not telling him about his drag persona, well that was no reason to feel guilty either.

Sasha watched him pace back and forth and took a sip of her wine. "I don't know why you're so agitated tonight." She always sat with him behind stage while he got ready. It was one of their traditions.

"Honey, have you not realized how big this night is for me? Devon is going to see me perform for the first time."

"Honey, have *you* not realized that he's probably seen you preform already, but he just didn't know it? What's the big deal? He loves you, so go out there and do your best."

"What if my best isn't good enough? What if I turn him off so much that he dumps me and we're quits?"

"Curtis, he. Loves. You." She held out her glass of wine. "You need this more than I do. I'll get another when show time starts. Come on now, take your medicine."

"I don't drink before a show, you know that."

"You need it this time around. Why do you think Devon will just run away? He didn't run when he saw you this morning, did he?" Sasha reached out and stroked his cheek, being careful not to mess up his make-up. "Now, come on, suck it back, doctor's orders."

Curtis did as he was told and downed the quarter glass in one go. He felt a bit of heat flare up on his cheeks. "Well, it's a good thing I'm a cheap date. I won't need blush now."

"There you go. Now you get yourself pretty. You're going on in a few minutes, you know."

"I know. Why do I feel like I'm on a first date?"

"Because you sort of are. Devon has never been properly introduced to Monica, has he? Go on. You will do beautifully. I know you will."

Nodding, Curtis adjusted his breasts, put a bit more blush on anyways and adjusted his wig. He looked fantabulous. He heard the announcer speak and his heart began to run a quick rhythm inside of his chest.

"All right everyone! Put your hands together for the birthday girl, Monica Diamond!"

Curtis went out onto the stage to yells and catcalls, applause and whistles. He waved at everyone and, when he saw Devon sitting front row centre, blew him a kiss. Devon caught it and blew one back to Curtis.

Seeing him there filled him with all kinds of feelings. Curtis hadn't really been sure that Devon was going to show up. Curtis wouldn't have blamed Devon if he hadn't shown up, he had really bungled the whole thing. The fact that Devon *had* shown up filled him with warmth that spread throughout his body.

He looked at the audience and smiled, taking a curtsey or two. He brought his microphone up to his mouth and spoke. "Thank you everyone! It's not easy turning twenty years old, but you make it all so fabulous."

The crowd laughed, knowing he was way older than twenty. "Tonight, there is a very special man in the audience. A man I love very much. I'd like to dedicate this first song to him. Maestro, if you please?"

The opening bars of *I Will Always Love You* began to play and Curtis took that moment to look down at Devon. He was smiling up at him, looking all handsome and sexy, and Curtis fell a little bit more in love.

Chapter Sixteen

Romilda always got a happy little thrill when she entered the GLBTQ Library.

When she had taken over the running of it from Prudence Gladwell, the place had been a quaint and serviceable library...that hardly anyone used or visited. When Romilda had first visited it, the library had reminded her of the library she had in high school, all grey walls and boring books.

She had immediately started putting more books on the shelves. She could not believe, for instance, that the library didn't have any books by Armistead Maupin. What gay library was complete without his books?

Next, she added Clive Barker's entire body of works. Some people objected over that, but she held firm. "He is a gay man and one hell of a writer. He deserves to be here as much as Oscar Wilde does."

Romilda had gone on to add Joseph Olshan's *Clara's Heart* and The Night Swimmer and the novels by Steve Kluger as *Almost Like Being In Love* was one of her favourite books of all time. She had read it more than ten times. She wanted to go beyond what people thought of as gay or lesbian literature. She had had enough of feminist poetry and gay tirades. Sure, feminism and tirades had their place, but when she wanted to sit down and read a good book, all she needed was a glass of wine, a comfortable chair and good lighting. All the drama could get the fuck out.

When she wanted to read, all she wanted was some nice music and the sound of the pages turning. Lately, people had come in asking if the GLBT Library lent out electronic books. She had laughed. "How do you expect me to lend out a book that doesn't really exist?" She had been shocked to learn that the public library had done this for years.

Romilda had been inspired. She had raised funding to have a whole computer system installed and had taken courses on how the whole electronic book thing worked. She wanted to give her clients, her readers, as much of a chance to read what they wanted when they wanted. That's what drove her.

When she came in that morning with Gaston, she was delighted when he looked around the place at all the people and smiled. There were families with kids, older folks with their grandchildren. There were kids listening to music by gay and lesbian artists or GLBT friendly songs. It amazed her. They had come from a place of battle to belong and were now in a time of acceptance; at least she hoped so.

Gaston looked like he was a kid in a candy store. "This is a marvelous place you've built Romy. A marvelous place. Say, I should read one of these books!"

"Oh, you don't have to do that."

"No, I should! This would be a way to support you!" He reached onto the returned books cart and picked up a book called Urinal by John Greyson. She took the book from his hands. "Oh, no honey, you're not ready for that one. Here," She handed him a copy of Tales of the City by Armistead Maupin. "This is a better place to start. We'll save that one for when you've read a bit more."

Blaine and Justin came into the main area where the sign out desk was. They both looked rather grim. They approached her cautiously, as if afraid to wake a sleeping dragon.

"Boys! What's wrong? You both look like your walking around on egg shells. What's gong on?"

"Well, we don't know how to tell you this," Blaine began.

"We just found out when we arrived for our shift today," Justin said.

"Found what out?" Romilda didn't like the sound of this.

Blaine took a slip of paper out of his pocket. Its yellow colour was cheerful and bright, even if it did contradict the bold-faced type on the sheet. Romilda took it out of Blaine's hands and looked at what the paper said.

Chapter Seventeen

There was no easy way to say it. So, Rebecca decided to just come out with it. She had made Dillon coffee and eggs and she was feeling very Martha Stewart. Perhaps that's why she said it. The only other excuse was that she was still drunk from the night before and, in thinking about it, this was a distinct possibility. She took a sip of coffee.

"So, here's the thing," She said, sitting down her coffee and then picking it back up again...and putting it back down.

Dillon put down his own mug of coffee. "Is there something wrong?"

"Nooo, why do you ask?"

"You're acting so weird. Like you're smiling before you've had your first cup of coffee. That never happens."

"Shut it, it does too happen. Like when we have morning sex."

Dillon gave her a wry look. "The last time we had sex early in the morning, you told me you wanted to take a coffee break."

"I stand corrected. But I'm okay. I've just been thinking about something I'd like to talk to you about."

"Okay."

"I think we should adopt."

Dillon choked on his coffee and spit out a mouthful on the kitchen table. "What?" He patted himself dry with his robe. "But you've never given an indication that you want kids, or anything and that's a big responsibility."

"What?" It was her turn to give Dillon a wry look. "I don't want kids."

"But you just said you wanted to adopt."

"I do, but not a kid, Jesus. I can barely take care of myself. I'd like to adopt a pet, like a dog or a cat or something."

"Shit, don't do that to me. Be more specific next time."

"Honey, you should know me by now. Kids like me fine, I don't like them too much. I like kids best when I can give them back. No, I was thinking a pet. I have a lot of love to give. A lot of it. I spent so long pining after your brother that I think I filled myself too full of love, you know?"

Dillon sighed. "Please don't bring him up so early in the morning. And what about me?"

"Oh, I love you with almost all of my heart. I have to keep a bit for myself, you know. But there's a little bit left over. I'd like to give that to a pet, give them a chance at a better life."

"You don't love me with all of your heart?"

"I love you with seventy percent of it, myself with twenty-five of it and that leaves five percent left over. I want to give that to something, you know?" She took a sip of her coffee.

"What about your family?" Dillon asked.

"What about them?"

"You don't have any love for them? Or for your friends?"

"Oh, honey, they wrote me off a long time ago. My only friend is Devon. I have no love for my family and they don't have any for me."

Dillon took another sip of what was left of his coffee and watched Rebecca as she got breakfast ready. She wasn't being honest with him. Why would her family just write her off? He had to find out and, hopefully, find something to take away that look of pain in her eyes.

Chapter Eighteen

Connie Collins, AKA River Moon Falls, was worried.

She had never seen William like this. He sat across from her, holding his bagel as if it held the voice of God. He just stared at it, saying nothing.

They had struck up an odd kind of friendship after what had happened with David. *I guess saving someone's life makes people friends*, Connie thought.

It had been odd at first. They hadn't really known each other before Connie had stopped William from killing David. At first, their friendship was stilted and somewhat awkward. Connie kept trying to bring him out of his shell though. She knew that what he needed was healing and he wouldn't heal locked away behind a closed door, hiding from the world.

It had been tough going at first. "Why won't you just leave me alone?" He asked all the time.

"Because I fucking care," she had said. "So should you."

Begrudgingly, he had grown stronger and the shadows under his eyes had faded. Connie knew what it was like to deal with abuse. She had been abused a lot by a lot of people. Eventually she had just gotten angry at the world and pushed everyone away.

She wouldn't do that with William.

Eventually, they had begun to trust each other. She knew that he was a recovering drug addict and victim of abuse. He knew that she was a ball busting lawyer and had no friends or relationship and was alone. Knowing the worst thing about someone when you start a friendship makes it easier to be friends, Connie thought.

"Hey William?"

"Huh?"

"William!" Connie snapped her fingers in front of William's eyes. He focused on her. "Finally! Honey, you okay?"

"Yeah. Why?"

"Well, because you're looking at your bagel like it's the mirror from Rompa Room. Did that bitch never say your name either?"

Connie was startled by the laugh that came out of him. He looked at Connie and smiled, setting the bagel down. "I'm sorry, I'm a bit out of it, I guess."

"What's up? You're not here."

"What do you mean?"

"Well, I was going on and on about how horrible Madonna was and you didn't say anything."

"Madonna is a Goddess." William said, squeezing his bagel.

"Yeah, which is why I knew you weren't paying attention. What gives, honey? Something is in your head and it sure as hell ain't the dulcet tones of my voice." She sighed and took another sip of her coffee and lit a cigarette.

"I'm eating here."

"You've been making love to that bagel for half an hour. I'm having a cigarette and you're going to tell me what's wrong."

"Nothing's wrong." He sighed. "Everything is wrong."

She tried to keep the sarcasm out of her voice. "Well, which is it, Willy? What's up?"

"I met someone!" he blurted out.

"William that's fantastic! Which app did you meet him on? Tinder, Grinder?"

"No app."

"So which site was it. Plenty of sausage? Thehappygayforest.com?"

"Nope, we met at a bar."

"A bar?" Connie scrunched her face in confusion. "Do people still do that anymore?"

William sighed. "We met at a bar."

"So, name, details, inches, tell me. I don't have anyone in my life, so I'm going to live vicariously though you. I'll just pretend that you're talking about someone with a vajayjay."

"His name is Zack. Oh, Connie, he's perfect. Red hair, green eyes, a smile that won't quit. He's funny and sweet and wonderful." He threw up his hands in despair.

"I'm failing to see what the problem is."

"He walks with a cane."

"So?"

"So, I didn't find out until we were leaving the bar. Why didn't he tell me?"

"Why is it any of your fucking business?"

"What do you mean?"

"Well, you met a stranger in a bar. It's not up to him to tell you everything about himself right away."

"Well, maybe there's something wrong with him. I should know before we go on a date."

"And that right there, ladies and gentleman, is why he didn't tell you he had a cane. It's none of your fucking business anyways."

"You think he's dealt with this before?"

"I guarantee it."

"Fuck, fuck, fuck. I bet he wasn't even drunk!"

"Okay honey, you lost me again."

"He had trouble with his balance. I kept teasing him about being drunk and he got really pissed at me. Kept yelling about not being drunk. He gave me his card and ran off. That was the other night. I don't know what to do."

She pulled out another cigarette and lit it. "Honey, let me get this straight…no, we don't do straight very well. Let's look at this in a slightly curved way: He was walking with a cane and had problems with his balance. And you thought he was drunk? No wonder he was fucking pissed at you, you fucking douchebag."

"Don't call me a douchebag."

"Douchebag, shithead, asshole. Take your pick."

"Why are you being so mean to me?" William whined, pouting.

"Because you're being an ass," Connie said. "Willy, did you ever think of just asking him what was wrong when he yelled at you that he wasn't drunk?"

"No, well, I thought that's all it was, you know?"

"So what are you going to do now?"

"Me? Why me?"

"Ball's in your court, handsome. He gave you his number, didn't he?"

William took the paper with Zack's number out of his walled. "Yes, he did." William wondered if he rubbed the number, if it would work like a talisman.

"Well, do you like him?"

"Yeah."

"Did you kiss? Was it good?"

"Yes, and oh God yes."

"Then it's up to you. But I'd call him. I haven't ever seen you gaga over a guy." She took a sip of her coffee. "I have to say, it looks good on you."

Chapter Nineteen

Romilda was afraid to look at the paper.

Even the colour felt loud. Yellow. Why couldn't they give out notices in a nice dusty rose, or bubble gum pink? What was the problem with that? It would make whatever news that was about to be delivered easier to handle.

She looked at Blaine and Justin. "Did you read it?"

Blaine looked down and scuffed his feet. "It was pretty hard not to."

She harrumphed. Loudly. "Why they insist on leaving official notices where anyone can see them is beyond me. Downright rude, if you ask me, which they haven't. Bastards."

She looked down at what the paper said:

OFFICIAL NOTICE

City officials have decided to demolish this building due to lack of funding.

Demolition will begin on April 30th.

Signed

Eldecot Johnsen, Mayor

Romilda's hands shook when she was done reading what was on the paper. Yellow, she thought, like a fucking lighting bolt.

"That fucking son of a bitch," she said.

"The mayor? Do you know him?" Blaine asked.

"Yes, I fucking know him. I know him well."

Gaston looked concerned. "Well, do you think he will help us?"

"Us?" Romilda spat.

Romilda turned to look at him and all Gaston saw was fire. He didn't back down. "Honey, of course. We're in this together. All of us, if you'll have me."

Justin gave him a wry smile. "Oh honey, you're gorgeous. You'll improve our little quartet in leaps and bounds."

Taking in all of Gaston, Romilda's gaze softened. "I'm sorry. I just get so angry when people are shits for no other reason than to be an asshole."

"Well, maybe the building is unsafe or there's another reason for the demolition?" Blaine asked.

"Oh, there's a reason for it, all right. Fucker thinks he can threaten me? He doesn't know who he's messing with, does he?"

The three men looked at her with open mouths. Gaston finally closed his and asked "Why would he be threatening you directly if he means to demolish the building?"

"Oh, trust me, this is about more than the building. I'm going to go see him."

"I'll come with you." Gaston said.

"I will, too, so will Justin."

She looked at all of them and felt only love for all three of them. Her heart was full with love for they would defend her in such a way.

"It's all good boys. This asshole calls for a woman's touch, I think. Now, would you look at that? A library full of people with no one to serve them. Let's go boys!"

As she sashayed away, Blaine said "I would not want to be on the receiving end of whatever she's planning. Whatever it is, it looks like it'll be devious."

"Yeah, but she sure is gorgeous when she's pissed off, isn't she?" Gaston asked wistfully.

Chapter Twenty

Curtis was trying to calm himself. He was a jumble of nerves and was still fretting after his brunch with Sasha. His thoughts revolved around Devon and the mess that he had gotten himself into. He didn't know if last night had made it worse or any better.

He composed himself in the mirror. When Devon had called and said that he had wanted to see him, Curtis had immediately thought the worst. He said sure and they agreed to meet up later today, but the whole time Curtis had his heart in his throat. *Here it comes,* he thought. *This is where he dumps me.*

Curtis didn't know why he was always jumping to the worst possible outcome, but he couldn't help it. All of his experience with men had conditioned him for this. He was just waiting for the axe to fall at this point. He had screwed everything up.

There was a knock on his apartment door and he opened it to find Devon standing there, holding a bouquet of roses. His mouth fell open in shock. Then the tears started to fall.

"Well, that's not usually the reaction a person expects from presenting flowers, but are those tears of happiness? I'd take those." Devon joked.

"Oh my God, Devon. You shouldn't have, you didn't need to."

"Actually, I did. It's what a boyfriend does when they go to see their boyfriend perform. I thought it was a theatrical tradition to give someone flowers after a performance."

Curtis began to sob in loud, hiccupping gasps.

"Look, I'll come in, Okay? I'll put these in some water."

"Oh, gosh, come in, come in. I'll find a vase." Curtis stepped aside and let Devon enter. "Did you want anything to drink?"

"You focus on the vase and the water and I'll focus on the drinks, okay?"

"Okay," Curtis said and he began to look for a vase. He wondered why Devon was here, why he had come. Surely flowers were an indication that he was breaking up with him? He took a deep breath and followed that up with a few more.

"Are you okay, Curtis? You sound like you're about to have a baby."

"I'm okay, I'm okay. Why, don't I look okay?"

"Actually, no. What's wrong?" Devon set the two glasses of wine back on the counter and took the vase from Curtis. He went to the sink and filled the vase with water and then put the roses in the water after cutting a bit off from their stems. "I thought of getting you a dozen, but figured two dozen was safer. It had more oomph that way in a vase, don't you think?"

Curtis nodded and felt a tear slide down his cheek.

"Honey, what's wrong? Did I do something?"

"No, no, it's all me. But first, I need to tell you something."

"Okay, I'm listening."

"Okay." Curtis took a deep breath. Then another. "I have shown you every side of myself. You've seen the me side, and the Monica side. I know that I should have told you about her before but was so worried about what you'd think."

"I think she's gorgeous."

"So, I completely understand...what?"

"You moved across that stage with verve and vigour. You knew all the words and you performed that song with more heart than I've seen any other drag queen do. I actually believed it was you singing instead of Dolly Parton."

"Oh." Curtis blinked a few times. "The thing is that I've shown you all of myself. Everything. And I love you."

"I love you, too."

"I don't mean in the nice fuckbuddy way, I mean in the I love you with all my heart and soul lets get married kind of way," Curtis said.

"I know. I love you that way, too."

"So...so these aren't break up flowers?"

"No, they're not. They're a way of showing you how much I love you."

Curtis started crying again. "I'm sorry, I'm such a blubbering idiot!"

Devon came closer to Curtis and wrapped his arms around him. "You're not an idiot. You spent your life afraid that men would never accept you."

"Then why do you?" Curtis asked. "Why do you love me?"

"Because you're honest and true and one of the most wonderful men I've ever met. And I've often felt the same way as you do."

"What? That men wouldn't accept you? You, a sex god?"

"Yeah. Me. Most men all they saw was the sex god, as you put it. They didn't see the real me. But you do. You always have."

"Oh, well, okay then."

"Now, are the tears done? Because we have wine to drink and I'd really like to get you naked. Is that okay with you?"

Curtis looked at Devon, at his rough and tumble good looks, at his dark curly hair and the stubble on his chin. "The wine can wait," Curtis said.

Chapter Twenty-One

They had arrived in Montreal with lots of time until the signing.

Nancy was still nervous and worried and everything in between. He put his t-shirts in the underwear drawer and his underwear in the bathroom. Michael watched Nancy wandering around the suite as if lost in a dream for a few minutes and then he took Nancy's travel kit out of his hands and put it on the bed. Then he pulled Nancy into an embrace and kissed him.

When Mike ended the kiss, he looked at Nancy and then ran a thumb over Nancy's lips. "Do you want to tell me what's going on?"

"Nothing. I'm okay. Did you know I'm a published author?"

"Yes, Babe, that's why we're here in this fabulous suite with a bath tub big enough for two and a king-sized bed and pillows that look like clouds, but you haven't remarked on any of that. What gives?"

Nancy told his heartbeat to slow down, that Mike was not his mother, that Mike wasn't mad at him. "It's my mother."

"You mentioned that on the train before you went all weird. What gives? You've never mentioned her before. I thought she had passed on."

"No. Sometimes, it's like she has, though. I haven't spoken to her in almost ten years. So, it really is like she's dead to me. Or I'm dead to her."

"Why would your mother not talk to you for almost ten years? How old were you when she stopped talking to you?"

"I was nineteen."

"God, such a young age."

"She had her reasons."

"What were they?" Mike asked.

"You don't want to hear about all of that."

"I learn you have a mother for the first time in all the years I've known you and now she's here and you're about to see her again for the first time in ten years?" Mike let out a soft laugh. "You can bet that I want to hear all about that."

Mike went to the mini bar and pulled out two bottles of Jameson whiskey. He poured two tumblers full of the amber coloured liquid and handed a glass to Nancy. "Now drink up."

Nancy nodded and took a big swig of the whiskey. He let out a breath. "Smooth but packs a punch. Thanks Babe."

"It's all good. It's what I'm here for. Now, why don't you tell me why a mother would stop talking to a man as gorgeous as you? Surely she'd love to have a son like you?"

"Well, she won't talk to me because I'm gay."

"What?!" There was shock in Michael's voice.

"That's not strictly true. I came out when I was nineteen. It was a hard decision, but my mother ended up being happy about it. She said that she now had a daughter and a son and that gay children were wonderful fashion accessories."

Mike looked slightly ill. "That's kind of horrible."

"I know, but at least they were okay with it, you know? It could have been so much worse. I had so many friends that were kicked out of home when they came out of the closet. The fact that she was thrilled was a good thing."

"So, what changed?"

Nancy took a deep breath. "My father came out of the closet two weeks later."

Chapter Twenty-Two

Cassie's eyes were swollen and red in the morning, which somehow made her look even more beautiful. Sebastian knew that she had suffered a personal loss, but it seemed to have turned her into an adult overnight.

"How are you honey?" Sebastian asked.

She shrugged. "I'm holding it together. Chuck brought me a chocolate cake and that helped."

"Is there anything I can do?" He asked.

Shrugging again, she went to the fridge and took out the chocolate cake. "You can eat this with me so I don't feel like a fat pig for eating all of it."

Smiling, Sebastian ruffled her hair. "Okay. I'm happy to. But then afterwards, I make you a real breakfast, okay?"

"Okay."

They sat at the kitchen breakfast bar with a plate of cake and two forks. They ate a few bites and enjoyed the silence that was always comfortable between the two of them. When Sebastian had been her mother, Cassie had enjoyed seeing how long they could go without talking. They could communicate everything with a simple look or with a nod of a head. Sebastian had always taught her to enjoy the silences.

It was only when everything was quiet that she would be able to find herself.

Eventually, Cassie spoke. "I'm sorry, pops."

"What do you have to be sorry about?"

"I'm sorry. I'm sorry Geoff is an asshat. I'm sorry he doesn't understand. I'm sorry there are people like him in the world." She took another bite of cake. "You must have gone through a lot. Like, a lot of people not understanding why you did what you did."

He nodded. "I did. It was hard. Thankfully, your father understood. He kind of always knew, anyway. He was my protector through out all of that. Transitioning isn't easy, but he made if easier."

Cassie nodded. "He is pretty cool. He's helped me through lots of shit."

"How is he?" Sebastian said hesitantly. "How is Kevin?"

"He's good. He misses you."

"I know. But I had to make a clean break, you know?"

"I do, a fresh start. Plus, Chuck is pretty hot. What does he do, bench press station wagons?"

Sebastian smiled a deep smile. "He does have nice guns, doesn't he?"

"Eeew, stop, you're giving out that horny look." She let out a laugh when Sebastian reached out to tickle her.

"Okay, I'll stop, I'll stop!"

The sound of her laughter turned in a second to the sound of crying. She put down her fork and put her hands to her face. Sebastian stood and held his daughter, trying to communicate everything in that hug.

"It'll be okay, honey. It'll be okay."

"No, you don't understand, dad." She said through sobs. She sobbed again for a few minutes and then spoke again in a hot whisper filled with sorrow.

"I'm pregnant."

Chapter Twenty-Three

Joe tried to remember that the doctor was here to help him. He tried to think positive thoughts and that everything was okay.

He also knew that was bullshit.

Joe knew the truth. He could feel it inside his body. It was an odd thing to live with something inside you that was literally eating you away, a little bit at a time. He felt it most within his lungs; once so strong and virile, they were now weak and unable to hold a breath for very long. He had been coughing a lot lately, so he knew it was getting worse.

He was living on borrowed time.

Joe looked up when the door opened. Dr. Carlisle came into the room, a soft smile on her face. "How are you feeling Joe?"

Grinning, Joe said, "I'm all right. I could be better though."

She sat down across from him and placed the folder she was carrying in her lap. She let it sit there. Though it was a plain blue folder, it seemed larger and heavier to Joe, as if it contained multitudes of possibilities.

Joe studied her face. Though it was fresh and she was a perfectly lovely woman, there was a heaviness to her features and a story in her eyes that she had been carrying around with her, one that she did not want to tell.

He reached for the folder. "Can I see the results?"

She nodded and handed him the file. "Though we had hoped that this experimental drug would halt the cancer or maybe even cure it, the drug didn't do a thing."

"I still don't see why we couldn't have done chemo."

"Joe, the cancer was too far gone when we found it. You knew that the medication was just a toss of the dice, a chance, a one in a trillion one." She placed a hand on his knee. "I'm sorry. Sorrier than you can ever know."

He nodded and that felt to him like he was agreeing on the weather instead of the fact that he was going to die. "How long do I have?" he said quietly.

"It's terminal, Joe. You could have anywhere between one month and six. I really can't say."

Joe felt his heart beat clutch in his chest. "I'm supposed to be getting married."

He saw a tear slid down Dr. Carlisle's face. "She must be a special woman."

"Oh, she is that. I've waited thirty years for her."

"Then don't wait a moment more. Does she know? About the cancer?"

Joe shook his head.

"Tell her, Joe. If you love her, tell her, the sooner the better." She stood and walked to the door. "I'll leave you for a moment to collect yourself."

Love and Lemonade

Dr. Carlisle had her hand on the doorknob when she turned back to Joe. "And marry your fiancé, Joe. We can all use a little love right now, okay?"

Joe nodded and, when she finally left and closed the door behind her, he let the tears come. He cried for every lost moment with Cordelia, for every moment that had now ben taken from them.

The tears slid down his face and into his cupped hands. He thought it was like catching his despair.

Chapter Twenty-Four

There was a loud knock on the door and someone yelled out "Anne of Avon Lady calling!"

Blaine answered the door with a large smile on his face. "Hey Poppy, how are you?"

She walked into the apartment and let Blaine close the door. "I'm good, but it's Dava I'm worried about."

"Come in, come in. Did you want anything to drink?" Blaine asked.

"You know, I'd love to have a cosmo, but it's a little early for me so I'll just have a glass of wine."

Blaine let out a chuckle and led the way to the kitchen. "I'll see what I can do." He took two glasses down from the cupboard.

"So, where's Justin?"

"He's out shopping with his mother. She got it into her head that she had to buy a new chandelier for our place for better light. Victoria said the light would show off my art."

Poppy took a look around the apartment. "It already kind of looks like a gallery. Would a little bit more light hurt?"

Blaine raised an eyebrow. "Said the woman who wants a glass of wine."

"I'll be good, I promise. So Victoria is still living here?"

Letting out a sigh, Blaine poured two glasses of red wine and passed one to Poppy. "Yes, she is. She's lovely in her way, but she always thinks she knows better. Justin just says its easier to go along with what she says."

"It's probably best. That woman frightens me."

Blaine laughed. "She's not that bad. She means well and she loves her son very much."

Poppy smiled and took a sip of her wine. "There is that."

"So, what's wrong with Dava?"

"Oh honey…" She took a deep breath. "I don't know. I have no idea how to help her."

"Has the cleaning gotten worse?"

"Yeah, it's like three times a day every day. She rarely lets me out of her sight and she goes to work and comes home, that's it. She's afraid all the time now."

"She went through a lot, Pops. "

"Yeah, I know, but I was the one that lost the baby," she spat out.

There was a beat of silence in the kitchen before Poppy said "Sorry."

"Why be sorry? It's the truth."

"Yeah, but that kind of makes me feel like an asshole. I know that she feels responsible for what happened, that Fred attacked us because she wanted the divorce. I keep telling her that she isn't to blame, that Fred is to blame and he's in prison where he belongs."

She paced the kitchen and then stopped, turning to look at Blaine. He saw pain in her eyes and could read the frustration off of her body.

"What do I do? What can I do? How do I bring back the woman I fell in love with?"

Blaine took a sip of his own wine before speaking. "Do you remember when I used to wash my hands all the time? Until they were cracked and bleeding?"

"Yeah, back when you were with David. You used to arrange the pictures on the wall and the books on your shelf, too."

"They were things I could control when my life was out of control."

"But her life is perfect now! We're still together, we love each other, Fred is in prison. We're all okay."

"People grieve in different ways. Maybe she needs a way to assert control over her own life, set her own boundaries."

"Yeah, that sounds good, but how do we do that?"

Blaine thought for a moment and said, "Have you ever thought of BDSM?"

Poppy was taken aback. "Bondage, Domination, Sadism and Masochism. You can't be fucking serious."

"Yeah, I am. It's a great way for people to feel safe and to establish control which is something that Dava desperately needs. There are a lot of clubs all over town that are safe places. I know you're not into that kind of thing, but maybe Dava would be."

Love and Lemonade

"I don't know, Blaine...."

"Here," He grabbed a piece of paper and wrote a number on it. "This is a number for a friend of mine. Tell Kaitlin I gave you her number. The least you could do is call her and see what happens. It might be just what Dava needs." He placed the number in Poppy's hands and wrapped his around them. "Just call her, Okay?"

Poppy nodded and gave Blaine a reassuring smile. "I will. I would do anything for Dava."

"I know." Blaine said and pulled her into a hug.

Chapter Twenty-Five

Nancy reminded himself that there was a possibility that she wouldn't come tonight. That his mother wouldn't show up and would be too angry or too afraid to see him. He was actually afraid of seeing her in public with ten years of words left unsaid.

"I still don't see why your mom is mad at you," Mike said. "I mean, you had nothing to do with your dad coming out of the closet."

As they got ready to leave their hotel room, Nancy tried to explain his mother's side of things. "You have to understand, Babe. I mean, not only am I not going to give her the grandbabies that she always wanted, her husband, her rock, wanted to leave her and start a new life."

"It happens all the time. I mean, look at what happened with Romilda and Cordellia. Look what happened with Sebastian."

"Yeah, but you haven't met my mother."

"No, I haven't."

Nancy sighed. "Look, I'm sorry that I never told you about her, I really am. But she's not in my life anymore.

"She's still your mom. She's still alive, she raised you. Is there anything else that you haven't told me about?"

Nancy gave him a nervous grin. "I have a boudoir set of sleepwear made out of gold lame?"

Mike smiled back. "You do not. You always say how gold lame is the lowest moment of fashion and everything else has had to try higher to shine because of it."

Nancy looked sheepish. "I do say that a lot, don't I?"

"Yeah you do." Mike pulled Nancy close and kissed him softly. "Don't keep anything else from me, okay? I love you completely but to do that properly, I have to know everything about you."

"Even about the hamster I had when I was a kid? How I named him Mr. Jingles and made him tiny Jackie O outfits that he could wear?"

"You had a crossdressing hamster?"

"Sure, didn't everyone?"

Mike kissed him again. "I love you, Clarence."

Nancy stared at Mike in fake horror. "You promised never to call me that! How could you?"

Mike laughed long and then kissed him one final time. "Come on, let's go. It won't be that bad. You always said how you wanted to be adored by masses of people. Now here's your chance."

"Oh, honey, I hardly doubt anyone will show up for little old me."

"Don't under estimate yourself. Your book is amazing. People already love it. When they meet you, they will love it more."

They caught a cab out front of the hotel and were silent as they drove over. Mike held Nancy's hand and tried to give him strength. He knew, that with the worries about his mother and how the book was being received, that Nancy was high strung at the moment. He pulled Nancy closer to him and kissed his forehead.

They drew closer to the bookstore and Nancy took a deep breath. Whatever would happen, would happen. He just thanked his lucky stars that Mike was on this journey with him. His life was magical with him.

As they turned to the address that Melissa had given them, they saw a huge crowd outside the bookstore. "Oh my gosh, there must be a fancy pants author coming," Nancy said. "But why would they have two different authors on one evening?"

"Um, Nancy honey? Look at the books they are carrying. They are here for you."

Chapter Twenty-Six

William dialed Zack's number and tried not to be nervous. He had done this before and it wasn't his first time at the rodeo, not his first time at the corral…he had to think of better references. He had never liked westerns.

But still. His hand was actually shaking slightly. William didn't remember the last time he had been this nervous about a boy. He hardly knew Zack, but there was just something about him that stirred something in William. He wondered if it was the charisma mixed with the vulnerability that Zack had showed him.

William had been hurt, too. He knew that look in Zack's eyes as well as he knew the look that he had carried with him in his own eyes. They had stared back at him from the glass for so long. Thankfully, Mike, Nancy, Chuck and Poppy had helped. And there was Cordella. She had helped more than she knew. Over time, that hurt and frightened look had disappeared from his eyes. William was thankful to all of them for what they had helped him through.

William wondered if Zack had someone in his life that he could turn to when he needed help. He wondered if Zack would let William be that person?

He let out a sigh. He was getting ahead of himself, here. He waited for Zack to pick up.

"Hello?"

"Hi! Zack!" William was surprised by the warmth that spread through him when he heard Zack's voice. "It's Will! How are you? Did you get home okay?"

"Will?" He said. "You're actually calling me?"

"Of course I am. Why wouldn't I? I said I would."

Zack let out a laugh. "Well, you're one in a million then."

"What do you mean?"

"Oh Will, guys always say that they will call, but they never do. Not every guy wants to date a someone like me."

"What? A hot guy? What are you talking about?"

"Nothing, nothing." William heard Zack let out a rough breath. "So, what can I do for you?"

"Well, I was wondering if we could go on a second date?" William asked.

"Actually, we kind of need to go on a first one. I'm sorry I flaked out at the bar last night."

"You didn't flake out. It's all good."

"Why are you being so nice to me?" Zack asked. There was heat in his voice.

"Because I want to get to know you better. I like what I got to know the other night."

Zack scoffed. "Sure, right. Okay, why don't we meet up? In about an hour?"

"Why are you so angry all of a sudden?" William asked.

Love and Lemonade

Zack let out a breath. "I'm sorry. I really am. This is hard for me."

"You weren't having that much trouble the other night."

"Yeah, but I'd had a few drinks before you showed up."

"Ah, liquid courage. I know it well."

"Look, I'm sorry, okay? I really am. I like you, Will. I really do. Will you let me make this up to you?"

"Of course."

"Okay, so can we meet at Confederation Park? I know it's cold out, but all the leaves changing look pretty. Would that be okay? "

"Yeah, I'd love that. I can be there in twenty minutes."

"Okay." Zack paused. "I'm really looking forward to seeing you, Will."

"And I you, Zack."

William hung up the phone and held it for a moment as if he could feel Zack though the handset. He remembered the shape of his eyes in the bar, the light glinting off of them from across the table.

Sighing, William wondered what was wrong with him. One date with a guy and he was acting all moony?

He sighed again and his mouth broke out into a smile as he got ready. He quickly brushed his teeth and threw on a clean shirt and a spritz of cologne. Grabbing his coat, he headed out. The walk to Confederation Park wasn't long, but he actually found himself walking more quickly than normal.

It was as if he couldn't get there fast enough. As he walked, he wondered why that could be. The only thing he could think of was Zack. Beautiful Zack.

William was nearing the entrance to Confederation Park when he saw Zack. He was wearing a brown corduroy jacket and blue jeans. William had never seen anyone so gorgeous. He called out to Zack before he could stop himself.

"Zack!"

When Zack turned to locate the sound of the voice and William saw those gorgeous green eyes, he felt himself swoon a little bit. He walked faster and Zack walked over to meet him.

Then they were standing in front of each other, both slightly out of breath.

"Hi," William said.

"Hey," Zack said.

William leaned into him and kissed him, softly at first, but the kiss intensified as Zack kissed him back. William wrapped his arms around Zack and felt at home in the embrace. All too soon, Zack pulled away from the kiss, but he was just as breathless as William was.

They looked at each other for a moment and William tried to take in the language of Zack's face, the planes and lines and crevices of it. He ran the pad of his thumb along Zack's lips, already wanting to kiss him again.

"I don't know what you've done to me," William said.

"What do you mean?"

"I feel like a schoolboy again."

"Oh, I hope not. I don't date the young ones."

William let out a loud laugh and kissed him quickly. "I'm glad to hear that."

"Did you want to go for a walk?" Zack asked.

"Sure. Let's just wait a moment. Walking with a hard on in your pants is uncomfortable."

Now it was Zack's turn to laugh. He let out a loud guffaw and a snort and grabbed William's hand and pulled him along.

"C'mon peg leg Pete. We'll walk slow, okay?"

Chapter Twenty-Seven

It was the perfect dress.

Not that Cordellia was one to wear white, this being her second marriage and she was far from virginal, but here she was in Colette's, an upper scale boutique, looking at the most perfect dress. It was a soft, creamy white with lace on the bodice with hand done embroidery in silver. The embroidery ran all though out the dress and just made it shimmer. Cordellia looked at herself in the mirror and felt like a young girl again.

"What do you think honey?"

Blaine smiled as his mother did a little twirl on the podium. "You've never looked lovelier. Joe isn't going to know what to do with himself. Why didn't Joe come with you anyways?"

"What, and let the groom see the bride in her dress before the big day? I may be old but I'm not one to ignore tradition."

"What did you wear when you and…Romilda got married?"

Though Blaine tried to cover it, Cordellia had heard the pause as he tried to figure out what to call Romilda. She had become the person she was always meant to be but, first and foremost, Romilda would be Blaine's father.

Cordellia ran a hand along his cheek. "When I married your father, it was just a quick justice of the peace ceremony. I think I wore a cotton print dress in white with daisies on them. I had never felt so beautiful before."

"Well, you look beautiful now."

"Don't I know it! Not bad for an old broad. Still, it's rather expensive. I don't know if I should."

"Mom, you've been back to this store to try on this dress five times already."

"I know, dear, but I'm still not sure."

"Well, Justin and I have been trying to think of what to get you and Joe for a wedding present. How about we buy the dress for you?"

"Oh, I couldn't."

"Mom, we've tried on ten other dresses in five other stores. This is the dress. You look stunning in it."

"Yes, but it was the first one I tried on."

"You were just lucky."

Cordellia turned to look at Blaine instead of regarding him in the mirror. "What if Joe doesn't like me in this dress? What if the dress isn't right? It could ruin the whole day!"

Blaine was shocked to see tears appearing in her eyes and threatening to fall on the dress. He pulled out a Kleenex and dabbed at her eyes. "Hey now. Joe has waited thirty years for you. You could walk into the room wearing a paper bag and he'd marry you!"

She let out a rich guffaw. Looking at him, Cordellia smiled. "I guess I'm just being silly. He's just been so…moody lately. I just don't know what's wrong. He's so silent and quiet and barely talks. I'm not sure what to do."

"Well, you could ask him what's wrong. He'll tell you. I know he will." Blaine pulled Cordellia close. "All he wants is your happiness, Mom. That's all."

"You're sure?"

"Yeah. You should ask him if something's wrong though, talk to him."

"I've tried, when I do ask him what's wrong, he turns into a man with no words. It's like I'm talking to a brick wall."

"Well, what did you do when I did that to you growing up?"

"I don't remember."

"Sure you do! You used to dress up as different people and talk in funny voices. I'd barely last five minutes before I broke out laughing. "

A warm smile graced her face. "Gosh, how do you remember that? Do you think it would work?"

"It's worth a try. I know that I could never resist laughing when you talked in your Miss Grumpalot voice."

That smile went from warm to glowing. "Oh, I did enjoy that one."

"You could try that with Joe. I suggest you don't wear the mop head as a wig when you do it, though. Might give him the wrong idea!"

Chapter Twenty-Eight

Dillon had to find out what was wrong with Rebecca.

Well, more with her family life. I mean, a family didn't just cut you out of their lives, did they? What could have happened that they would have stopped talking to her? Parents were supposed to love their children…sometimes too much. Devon was a perfect example of that. His mother had loved his brother so much that she had ended up with nothing and would have gratefully given him everything else.

He loved his brother, he really did. In some ways, Devon was like the other half of him. Dillon just couldn't stand Devon and didn't want to be near him. If Rebecca wanted him to deal with Devon and the anger that lived between them, she had to deal with her family.

He had the sneaking suspicion that she would need help, though. Dillon thought about it and called Devon. He knew her best, they were best friends. So it would stand to reason that he would know what had happened or what was going on.

Dillon dialed Devon's phone number. He didn't know if Devon would pick up the phone, but had to hope that he would. Dillon had to know.

To Dillon's surprise, Devon picked up on the third ring. "Hey douchebag."

Laughing, Dillon said, "Hey shithead."

"Well, this is a first. I didn't think you'd ever call me for any reason, despite Rebecca urging us to talk."

"It's actually her that I'm calling about."

"Well will wonders never cease. What about her? Are things okay?"

"Yeah, they're good. Very good, actually. I just had a question. How long have you known Rebecca for?"

"About ten years or so."

"Did you ever meet any of her family or friends? Does she have any parents?"

"Yeah, but she doesn't talk to them."

"Do you know why?"

"No idea. I did meet an aunt of hers once, though. It was her aunt Josephine. She was really cool, apparently. Rebecca used to talk about her a lot and they would go shopping together."

"Does she still talk to her?"

"I'm not sure. Why do you want to know all of this?"

"Because of something that Rebecca said a day or so ago. She said that her family had written her off, that she only had you and me and that was enough."

He heard Devon let out a breath. "Well, I do know that they had a falling out of some kind. But I always thought they got back in touch. I wonder what they fell out about?"

"I don't know. Do you think that this aunt Josephine has the same last name as Rebecca? Daniels?"

"I don't know, but it's worth a shot."

"Listen, you can't tell her about this, okay? That I'm looking into her family and stuff."

"No problem. But why is it such a big deal to you?"

"Because I love her." Dillon paused and took a breath. "And I don't want what happened to us to happen to her."

"Oh." He heard Devon's shock in that one word. "Okay."

Dillon took another breath. "Rebecca tells me that you've met a new guy, a real keeper. Curtis?"

"Yeah. Yeah he's a keeper. He sees me for who I really am. There's nothing fake about him except his breasts."

"Okay, what?"

Devon laughed. "He's a drag queen part of the time. So he has fake breasts."

Dillon let out a loud laugh. "That must take a while to get used to!"

"Yeah, but I love him, so it's worth it. He's worth it."

"Good, you sound happy. He treats you well?"

"Yeah…better than I've been treated in a long time."

"I'm glad. I'm really happy for you, Devon."

"Thanks."

"Would you both like to come over for dinner?" Dillon couldn't believe he'd just said that. Did someone take over his mouth and brain? Rebecca had planted the idea in his head, he would just blame her.

"Are you serious? That would be awesome! I can't wait to see you Dillon, and you could both get to know Curtis better."

"I'd like that." He was surprised that it was true. "I'd like that a lot."

Chapter Twenty-Nine

Sebastian's world stopped moving.

His daughter, his baby girl, pregnant. He knew it was always a possibility, but he had pictured her married and happy, content with the world around her. Not like this, not wanting to hide from the world because of some asshole named Geoff had rejected him and therefore had rejected her.

This wasn't supposed to be the way it happened. Cassandra was supposed to be happy, she was supposed to be overjoyed. Added to that, Sebastian was supposed to be thrilled to be able to lend some wise words of parental wisdom. He wasn't supposed to want to find some faceless boy and beat the crap out of him.

Sebastian reminded himself (for the millionth time) that she was afraid and she didn't need to see his anger. That would come later.

Chuck made all of them tea. Cassandra laughed at him as he boiled the water and picked out some mugs and brewed the tea. "That seems like a very girly thing to do. I thought you were mister macho man! Look at you making tea!" She let out a giggle.

"My grandmother taught me about the joys of making tea. She always made it when we were upset or there was a problem to deal with."

"So now I'm a problem to deal with?" Cassie said.

"No, but tea is very healing. I'm making some camomile. It's good for calming the nerves and for depression."

Chuck hummed while he made the tea. Sebastian appreciated what he was doing. Chuck was trying to calm them all down, to keep them from losing it. He brought the tray filled with cups and saucers, the tea pot and a large plate piled high with cookies to the table in the living room and sat it down gently.

"Are those fig newtons?" Cassie asked.

"Yes they are."

"And those? Are those double stuffed Oreos?" She asked meekly.

"Why yes, they are."

"Those are my favourite cookies," Cassie said with a watery smile.

"I know. Now eat up while the tea cools a little bit. I made camomile tea. I made it like my grandmother taught me, so it's scalding hot."

He sat down across from Cassie and gave Sebastian a reassuring smile when he took a cookie from the plate on the coffee table. "So, Cassie. What's going on?"

She looked at him aghast. "You fucking know what's going on. I'm fucking pregnant."

"I know," Chuck said. "I was just trying to ease the tension." He took a bite of the cookie. "So how did this happen?"

"Look, I know you're gay and everything, but I assume you know how sex between a man and a woman works, right? "

"Oh, I know. I've seen pornos. I still get nightmares. Are you sure you don't have teeth down there?" He let out a little laugh at Cassie's shocked face. "There, that's better. You don't look like your face is going to melt off of you from sadness. Now, tell me what happened."

Sebastian was so thankful for Chuck at that moment. He was thankful every day for him, but never more so than that moment. He had never loved him more. As he took the time to calm his daughter, his heart opened up further. Sebastian had thought he loved Chuck completely, but at that moment, Sebastian's love for Chuck grew.

Cassie shrugged. "I don't know. It was just so fucking stupid. Everything was going all right. I had moved here to be closer to my dad, I got to be closer to Geoff. But he couldn't take it when I told him about dad, just couldn't imagine what that was about. I tried to tell him that dad held no baring over us, that it didn't matter. But he couldn't take it, didn't want to take it, was afraid of the idea, I don't know."

She took a cookie, a double stuffed Oreo, and bit into it. "He is such a fucking dumb ass. I mean, what was he afraid of? He actually asked me if transgenderism is catching, whether I'd get the urge to be a fucking man. As if I would get that urge, I love cock too much. But whatever, he was just fucking afraid!"

Cassandra had stood and crushed the half of the cookie that remained in her fist. As she shook her hand, little chocolate crumbs rained down from her fist. "Men fucking suck!" She didn't realize it, but she had gone from being weepy and sad to being angry. That was an improvement by Sebastian's way of thinking.

"Oh, they do," Chuck said. "Also, they smell terrible, have you ever noticed? When did you find out you were pregnant?"

The look on her face hardened. "Last night," She said. "I did the test. I haven't gotten my period for a while now."

"So have you told Geoff?" Chuck asked her. "He's the father right?"

Cassie gave him a scathing look. "Of course he's the father. I'm not a slut or anything."

Chuck gave her a wry smile. "Honey, there isn't anything wrong with being a slut. I used to sleep with anything that moved or was capable of breathing, you know. There's nothing wrong with being free with your body."

"Okay." She gave him a small smile and some of the anger faded from her face. "Thanks."

Giving her a smile in return, Chuck wondered how he was going to say what he had to say without sounding like an asshole but didn't see any way around it. "You should tell

Geoff about the baby so you guys can decide what you're going to do." He said quietly.

Her fists hardened to the point where her knuckles were white. The carpet was now a mess of cookie crumbs. "I'm not getting rid of my fucking baby."

Sebastian was ready to step in, but Chuck had it covered. "Of course not. No one is saying that. But if you two are having a baby, you have to decide what to do, how to be parents, that kind of thing. It didn't even occur to me that you would get rid of it."

She looked a little calmer and sat down, opened her hand and stared at the massacred cookie bits. "Oh. I see." She licked the chocolate off of the palms of her hands.

"You have to at least tell him, Cassie," Sebastian put in.

When she turned to look at him, Sebastian wasn't prepared for how grown up she looked. To him, she would always be his little girl. "I'm not telling him anything. He's a fuckwit pimple fart and I'm not telling him anything."

She let out a snort of laughter and took a sip of her tea and then reached for another cookie.

Chapter Thirty

As they began walking, William reached out and took Zack's hand.

Zack stiffened slightly. "You don't have to, you know. It's okay."

"I *want* to. Really."

"Why would you want me anyway? "

"Um, let's see. You're funny, you have a great sense of yourself and your hot as fuck. I want to get to know you, but it feels like you don't want to get to know me."

Pulling his hand away, Zack turned to William. "Oh, no, I want you more than anything. I want to be exclusive with you."

"Do you want to wear my pin, too?" William said with a grin.

Zack let out a laugh. "I only meant that there isn't anyone else in my life that I want to date. You're the only man I want."

"Glad to hear it." William took Zack's hand again. "Hey, where's your cane?"

Zack shrugged. "I don't need it today," he said.

"Are you sure? You don't have to be embarrassed about using it around me. My friend Connie told me that I was kind of an ass for saying that you were drunk last time we saw each other."

"Yeah, you kind of were, but then so was I. So all is forgiven."

"Zack, are you okay?" William stopped walking and took hold of both of his hands. A shower of leaves fell down around them and the air seemed to whisper. William saw Zack's fear. He could read it in his eyes. He wanted to pull Zack into an embrace, but knew that if anything between them was going to continue, Zack had to tell him what was wrong.

"Look, can we sit?" Zack pointed to a fountain. It had been emptied of water but the sun was shining and it wasn't terribly cold.

William nodded and they walked over to the fountain and sat down. William waited for Zack to speak, was desperate to hear his voice, wanted to urge him to speak. However, he knew that Zack had to speak in his own time.

Taking hold of one of Zack's hands, William gave it a gentle squeeze and looked up at Zack. William was surprised to see that he was crying.

"Look, I'm just going to say this. I'm terrified that you're going to run away screaming into the wind, and I wouldn't blame you. I really wouldn't. I mean, I've tried not telling men, and that didn't work out too well when I showed up to the date with my cane. And I've tried telling them beforehand too, so they knew what to expect. One of them thought I could be cured."

"God, Zack, are you dying?" William's voice came out in a whisper.

"No, nothing like that. Although, it's kind of like I did die and now I'm finding myself again. But I'm getting ahead of myself." Zack wiped at his eyes.

Zack turned and faced William and William prepared for the worst possible news.

Taking a deep breath, Zack spoke: "I have relapsing-remitting Multiple Sclerosis. I'm sorry."

"Why are you sorry?"

"Because I'm not perfect."

"You're wrong, you're perfect for me," William said.

"Why aren't you running away, screaming in terror? You're not afraid of me or treating me like I'm about to drop dead or something to be gawked at."

William let out a little laugh. "Why would I do that?" he asked. "My aunt had Multiple Sclerosis and she lived to the ripe old age of eighty."

Zack gasped in shock. "Oh, thank goodness!" Zack took in a huge gulp of air and let it out again. "You don't know how many men I have to explain it to." Letting out a sigh, Zack leaned into William.

William wasn't sure Zack was aware that he had done so, but he wasn't going to point it out to him. It was nice having

Zack this close. Zack was warm and the sound of him breathing so closely to his ear felt wonderful.

"What? So, people don't know what it is?" William asked.

"No, not everyone. There are some that think that since I'm taking pills that I'm cured. There are some guys that got grossed out at my having to take an injection every day; one guy compared it to taking heroin."

"How are they even remotely the same? One kills you and one makes you better." William shook his head. "People are good in theory. In practice, they kind of suck."

Zack started laughing. He leaned forward and William immediately missed his body heat. It wasn't a need to see him naked (though that did exist). It was more that Zack made William feel whole. He had never felt like that about another man before, not even Michael. Especially Michael.

"God, that's perfect. And so true. Thank you for that."

When William looked at Zack's eyes, at their brilliant green, flecked with brown and gold, he swooned a little bit. "Don't mention it. It's the truth." William reached for a hand so that he could feel Zack's heat again. "What do I need to know?"

Zack shrugged. "I'm a Leo, I have a fondness for Nintendo games that takes over a lot of my life. I read three to five books a week."

William gave Zack a bright smile. "Funny man. I meant about the MS. Is there anything that I should know?"

Zack shrugged again. "We can get to that. I assume this means that you don't find me frightening and you're not going to run away in fear, screaming for your soul?"

Letting out a hearty laugh. "Hardly. I could fall in love with you."

There was a beat of silence. Afraid he had said too much, William reached out for Zack's hand again. "I mean, um, well I meant what I said, but I don't want you to think that, um. Yeah."

Zack looked at William with eyes that were so full and open. William swore that he could see into Zack's soul. He wasn't sure how long they stared at each other but then Zack moved forward and kissed him.

William sensed something different about this kiss compared to the one they had had before. It was softer, deeper. It was also a slow kiss but didn't lack any fire. In fact, it made William harder than any other kiss he had ever experienced.

When Zack broke the kiss, he gave William a soft smile. "I should let you know that even though I have Multiple Sclerosis, I have perfect working order of my penis."

William let out a loud laugh and didn't think he had ever felt so good.

Chapter Thirty-One

Nancy walked forward as if in a dream.

Admittedly, he had always dreamed of something like this. What artist didn't dream of some kind of fame? Didn't they all create something to leave behind so that they had proof of their creativity? Like everyone else, they didn't want to pass away from the earth unknown.

It was more than that, though. He wrote not because he merely wanted to, though aside from kissing Mike, writing was one of his life's greatest pleasures. No, he wrote because he had to, he wrote because there were so many words inside of his body that if he didn't let them out, he'd go crazy.

He knew that he was writing for himself, that he needed to get the words down somehow, but the fact that his novel was out in the world in hardcover? That people were reading it? And it was being well reviewed?

That was priceless to him, like some kind of magical hat-trick.

There were hundreds of people here. Nancy had thought that he would show up to read from his book to an empty room and maybe sign one or two copies. The fact that there were so many people here to hear him was something close to amazing.

One of Melissa's publicists came up to him. "Charles! So nice to meet you! I'm Anna! I work with Melissa."

"It's Nancy, please."

"I can totally see you as a Nancy. There will be a different publicist joining you in every stop. Come with me, I can show your husband where he can sit and get you all set up." She gave him a bright smile.

"Are all these people here to see me?" He asked.

"Yes! Isn't this amazing? There are over three hundred people here! Melissa told me to mention that it looked like your book had moved up to the number three spot on the New York Times! Isn't that awesome?"

"That is so very awesome!" Nancy waved to the crowd who cheered when they saw he had noticed them.

Mike gave Nancy a squeeze. "I'm so proud of you."

"Thanks Babe."

"I'm honoured to be your husband."

A warmth gushed through him. They were husbands in all but the legal sense. "I'm honoured to be yours," Nancy said to him.

Anna led them into the store where more people were waiting. Nancy saw a table set up with copies of his book. The cover had been changed and New York Times Best Seller had been added at the top. There must be hundreds of copies.

Nancy grinned. Good thing he had strong wrists.

"You look like the cat that got the cream," Mike said jokingly.

"Remind me to tell you about it later."

Anna brought Nancy to the front of the store where there was a podium and a table with a pitcher of water and a glass. There was also a copy of his book sitting on the table. "Oh, I won't need that," Nancy said.

"But won't you need it to read out of?" Anna asked.

"No." He took a copy out of his bag. "I always keep the very first copy with me. Sort of like a good luck charm, you know?"

Anna showed Mike where to sit. He was in the front row. Nancy kissed Michael quickly before more people started coming in. "I love you," he said.

"And I love you," Mike said, then he went to take his seat.

Nancy tried to calm himself. Tried to tell himself that there was nothing to be nervous about, that writers did this all the time. He said a quick internal prayer to the Goddess of Fabulous Sparkle and opened his book up to the right spot.

Then he looked up into the audience. The first person he saw was his mother.

Nancy almost stopped reading right then. He almost lost his voice and would have had to crawl down within himself to find it, had she not given him a little smile. True, it was just a curve of the of her mouth, but it was a smile nonetheless.

He looked over at Michael as he read and could feel Michael's love and warmth for him. Though his mother smiled, he did not sense warmth in her gaze; merely curiosity. As he read, he tried to look at other people, tried to take in their faces, but his eyes kept being drawn back to his mother. She had barely aged in twenty years. Nancy wondered if she would still smell the same if he was lucky enough to hug her.

He read the first three chapters from *What's Love Got to Do with It?* and the crowd loved every word. They all clapped at the end of the reading. His insides were shaking and vibrating, and not in the good way. Nancy couldn't believe how nervous he was that she was here.

Nancy was given a chair at the table and he pulled out a fancy pen. He signed for what seemed like forever, but was in reality just over an hour. Anna said that the bookstore had asked him to sign the rest of the ones on the table and he agreed. Why anyone wanted his signature on anything other than a cheque was amazing to him.

He signed a book for a gentleman who told Nancy that his characters were so real, so vibrant. When he looked up and found he was the last person wanting a signature, he didn't see his mother anywhere.

Mike came up to him and hugged him, kissed him hard and quick. "You were amazing, Babe. So amazing. There were so many people! Who knew there would be this many?"

"I know, right?" He looked around for his mother.

"Nancy, that was phenomenal!" Anna said. "Now the next stop will be more of an interview and a signing, just to change it up a bit." She paused. "Nancy?"

Love and Lemonade

He saw her in the crowd of people leaving the store. She took one moment to look back at him, her eyes filled with tears, as she slid from the store.

Chapter Thirty-Two

"I still don't understand what we're doing here," Dava said.

Poppy looked up at the sign to make sure they were at the right place. It matched the name that Kaitlin had given her: *The Velvet Whip*. The name of the bar was written in gold leaf upon black wood. The doors were also dark and trimmed in gold leaf, giving the whole place a classy air. *This is a BDSM club?* She thought.

"Dava, I told you. This is a place that can help you. That can help us."

"What do you mean? Help me how?"

Shit, she thought. She should have talked to Dava about what kind of club The Velvet Whip was before bringing her here. Poppy had been afraid that she would not have wanted to come.

Turning around, Poppy saw a little café. It looked nice enough. Who knew that a BDSM club could be in such a nice neighbourhood? "Let's go for a coffee, Dava. I'll explain it over a drink and a cookie."

Dava gave her a smirk. "Make it two and we have a deal."

Love and Lemonade

Poppy had called Kaitlin the night that Blaine had given her Kaitlin's number. Poppy had been surprised by how normal Kaitlin had sounded. Poppy's only experience with BDSM was a brief time during her high school years when she had experimented with her Goth friends. It had been all about anger and doing what you were told.

Kaitlin sounded...well, like a normal well-adjusted woman. Not at all what Poppy thought a woman into BDSM would sound like. She pictured someone who lived in their parents' basement and got off on the sound of whips. Kaitlin sounded like a normal woman...except for the fact that she was into BDSM.

She had invited Poppy and Dava to the Velvet Whip so that they could check out the club and learn about BDSM and what it could bring into their lives. Poppy agreed, although not enthusiastically.

Poppy could wrap her head around a lot of things: Drag Queens, crossdressers, anal beads, the use of dildos, even those who liked to be peed on or pooped on...if you were into that, she didn't judge. She would never try it, though.

What Poppy didn't understand was people who would willingly hurt others for the sake of sexual enjoyment. That just boggled her mind. Why Blaine thought that Dava would benefit from all of this was beyond her, but Poppy was desperate. She had watched the woman she loved with all of her heart withdraw further and further within herself. If there was a way to get Dava out of herself again, however it was done, Poppy was all for it.

They ordered coffees (a latte for her and an americano for Dava) and three cookies. A waitress set them down and they were left alone.

Poppy broke the silence first. "Dava honey, you haven't been yourself."

Dava huffed. "I have to."

"Sweetheart, you hate to clean but that's all you do now."

"So? There's nothing wrong with cleaning. Maybe I'm a changed woman, huh? Ever think of that?"

"Dava, nobody cleans the kitchen three times a day," Poppy said softly.

A tear slid out of Dava's eye. "I know."

"And nobody cleans the bathroom twice a day."

"I know." More tears slid out of her eyes and slid down her cheeks.

"Dava, my love, what's wrong? You can tell me anything, you know."

"How can you ask that?" Dava said, her voice rising. "When I think of what happened to you, what you lost…"

"Dava, none of that is your fault. I've told you that before."

"Yeah, but Fred was my ex-husband! It's my fault that all of that happened. If I had just left well enough alone…"

"You would have been miserable. I would have been unhappy. Now at least we have each other."

"But the baby…"

"I know honey, I know." Poppy reached out and took Dava's hand. With her free hand, she wiped away a tear and then took a sip of her latte. "I think of her every day, you know. Every damn day. It's been months since all of that happened and sometimes, I can still feel her inside me."

Poppy put a hand on her stomach and rubbed it absentmindedly. She had been doing that a lot since the miscarriage had happened. She didn't know if she would ever stop. "There are times where I feel like part of me is missing."

"Then how do you do it? How do you go on?"

"I just do. I try to live every day to the fullest because I believe it's what she would have wanted." Poppy took another sip of her coffee. "Why do you clean all the time?"

Dava gave Poppy a look that said the answer should have been obvious. "Because it's something that I can control. I couldn't save you, I couldn't stop you from being hurt. I can clean. I can do that and maybe I will stop seeing all that blood." The last word came out in a whisper.

Poppy moved both drinks and took hold of both of Dava's hands. "You listen to me, Dava. You aren't responsible for what happened. I still love you and want to build a life with you. Maybe we both need this BDSM thing. Maybe it can heal both of us."

She gave Dava's hands a quick squeeze. "I love you more and more every day and hate to see you like this. Maybe it can help. What do you say?"

Dava nodded. "Yes, we will try it. But can we go after we finish the cookies?"

Poppy let out a loud laugh and realized it was the first time that she had laughed in a long time.

Chapter Thirty-Three

Blaine reminded himself that she was going to be his mother in law. He wasn't allowed to harm her, Justin would probably frown at that.

"I mean, darling, it's not that these paintings aren't powerful," Victoria waved a well-manicured hand at a series of paintings that he had done. The paintings featured homeless people he had seen around Ottawa. They were painted just as they are, some of them holding out their hands for money, some of them looking at the viewer with eyes so wide, you could almost see their souls. "I'm just saying are they necessary, darling? Do people need to see more homeless people? It's been done, it's so passé!"

She walked over to the other portraits, the one featuring Moira front and centre. "Now, these ones, they are of people that people will want hanging in their homes!"

"Victoria, I think you're wrong. I think everyone is valid, whether or not they have money."

"Yes, but Blaine, I really think that people would be offended looking at a bunch of homeless people."

"Shouldn't that be what great art does? Move people to feel some sort of emotion? If these paintings make you feel something, even disgust, then it means I've done my job as an artist."

The exhibit was shaping up wonderfully. The art cards had been printed and were lovely. Even in miniature, they sang to him. He had chosen almost all of the thirty canvases he was allowed to show in the exhibition. Blaine wanted to fill the last five spots with five canvases of his homeless people. There was something about them that just spoke to him and those were the canvases that Remmington Pecora had said she had wanted. She wanted his work to speak to others as they had spoken to her.

Blaine had chosen each piece carefully, making sure that each one of them sang to him. He thought that Victoria would be thrilled with all of his choices, but she had been full of nothing but criticism. None of the portraits, aside from Mo's, met her approval.

Her energy was frantic and manic as she paced around his studio. She seemed crazed and there was a wild look in her eyes. Sadness came off of her in waves. He wondered why he hadn't noticed it before.

Taking a deep breath, Blaine asked, "Victoria, what's wrong?"

She turned to look at him and Blaine saw that she was crying. Tears slid down her cheeks and she clenched her fists at her sides and shook them. "Nothing! Nothing is wrong!"

"Victoria, don't be silly! Tell me what's wrong?"

She turned from him then, as if she didn't want Blaine to see her pain. "He's found someone else!"

"Who?"

"My asshole of an ex-husband. The divorce papers have just been signed and he's already moved in a younger model! I thought we were going to be together forever!"

Blaine went to her and gently touched her shoulder. "You left him, Victoria. So you could be a mother to your son."

"Yes," she said. "Yes you're right. You're so right, Justin and you are everything to me."

"Well, then what's the problem?"

"I want him to suffer!" She almost screamed this out loud. "I wanted him to be a mess without me!"

"Well, you can do what every gay man does."

"What's that?"

"Find someone younger and more attractive."

She turned to face him with a bright smile on her face. "Oh, Blaine darling. That's a *marvelous* idea!" She had a mischievous gleam in her eyes. "Where does one find a man, Blaine?"

He looked at her in confusion. "I'm sorry?"

"A man! Where does one find one? It's been so long since I've dated anyone that I'm not really sure how to do it anymore. What kind of man would want someone washed up like me?"

"Oh Victoria!" Blaine didn't second guess his actions and went to her, wrapping her in a hug. "Don't ever say that. You are not washed up."

"That's nice of you to say, but you don't have to compliment me because you're sleeping with my son."

Blaine's mouth fell open in shock until Victoria grinned at him and laughed. "Oh, you should see your face! It's like you have been handed your balls on a silver platter! Delightful!" She cackled merrily. "Oh thank you Blaine! I needed that!"

Narrowing his eyes Blaine said, "Happy to oblige."

She squeezed his hand. "Really, thank you. Justin told me that you don't give compliments willy nilly. That when you give one, you mean it."

Blaine softened a little bit. "Well I do. You're not washed up. You're a vibrant woman with so much to offer any man lucky enough to capture your attention."

"Thank you Blaine."

"But you're also a bit of a bitch."

Victoria blinked in surprise and then let out a loud bark of a laugh.

Chapter Thirty-Four

"So, are you going to tell me what's wrong?"

Shit, Cordellia thought. She hadn't meant to come right out and say it like that. They had been making dinner and Joe had been grumpy all evening. She had made him his favourite foods tonight to see if she could cheer him up: steak and fresh bread, green beans with butter and some baby potatoes. She had grilled all of this on the barbeque and had plated it nicely. Martha Stewart would have been proud. Well, maybe not. Martha Stewart was a little stuck up.

She had placed the plates down on her dining room table that she had laid out with her best table cloth and had lit white candles and had put on some soft music. None of that Yani new age crap. Just some lovely Enya music instead.

When it was all done, she had gone to the living room and found him staring at a book, but not reading it. "Honey? Dinner is ready."

He had nodded and had followed her to the dining room. He was shuffling his feet, looking utterly defeated. It was as if all the life in him had left him and she was left with a husk of a man, neither alive nor dead.

Instead of his normal chivalrous self, always the gentleman, he just sat at the table. She set his plate in front of him and he didn't say anything. She stood looking at him for a few minutes and there was no reaction from him at all. Nothing. He just sat there looking more and more lost within himself.

"So, are you going to tell me what's wrong?"

When she barked the words at him, Joe looked up and was astonished to see that he was crying. Not just a few tears, but a waterfall of tears. She wondered if he would be able to stop the tears, or if they would continue coming forever.

"Oh, Joe, what is it? What's wrong?" She went to him and pulled him into an embrace, tried to hold him together as he quietly fell apart. Cordellia didn't know what to do except hold him and whisper to him how much she loved him and that, whatever this is, whatever was causing this upset, they would see their way through it.

"But that's just it," he said hoarsely. "There is no way through it, none. They've tried, I've tried, but there's nothing they can do for me."

"Joe, what is it?" Cordellia asked. She took him and sat him down on the couch.

"What about your lovely dinner?" he asked. "Everything will go cold."

"I don't give a donkey's ass about the dinner. We can heat it up. Now will you tell me what's wrong with you? Tell me how I can help?"

Love and Lemonade

"You can't help me," he said. When Joe looked away, she knew that it must be bad. If he couldn't look at her, it must be horrible.

Taking a deep sigh, Joe took one of Cordellia's hand in both of his. When he finally did turn to look at her, she saw that the tears he had cried had dried on his face, making it look as if he were made of glass and would break at any moment.

"I have cancer," he said.

"Oh, Joe! Well, there's lots of treatments nowadays, lots of things they can do to put it in remission," Cordellia said.

Joe shook his head. "It's stage four prostate cancer. The doctors have done everything that they can possibly do."

Cordellia was quiet for a moment. She knew that he didn't need hysterics. All Joe needed at this moment was love.

"Well then," she finally said. "How soon do you want to get married?"

She could tell that shocked him. "You couldn't possibly want to get married now. The doctors don't know how long I have. It could be one month, it could be six, but the end is the same."

She took his hand now and looked at him. "Now you listen to me, Joseph Gabriel Andrews, we have waited thirty years for each other. There is nothing, I repeat nothing, that will stop me from marrying you. Okay?"

Joe gave her a little smile. He always did like it when she talked like a drill sergeant. "Okay," he said.

"All right then. So, I repeat: How soon do you want to get married?"

Chapter Thirty-Five

Poppy wasn't sure what she expected inside The Velvet Whip, but it wasn't a luxe club with soft jazz playing in speakers that she couldn't see. She was nervous and was trying very hard to find something to be judgemental about.

The room they had walked into looked like a sea of glass, but it was really black marble shot through with veins of white, gold and silver. There were fire places ablaze with flames in the back of the room. Poppy saw elegant red velvet couches and black leather chaise lounges. There were people sitting at the bar and at one of the low tables, reclining in leather chairs.

She looked at Dava who was taking it all in herself. She let out a low whistle. "I didn't know that it would be so…" She took a moment to think of the right word. "Classy? This is so not what I was expecting. When you said S and M, all I could think of was the red room from fifty shades of grey." Dava shivered. "This looks like a fucking commercial for happy hour at some swanky club."

They walked slowly into the club, holding each others' hands. Poppy didn't know how Dava was feeling at this moment, but Poppy certainly got some courage from Dava and being able to feel her heart beat through her hand.

"I love you," Poppy said.

"And I love you," Dava said.

They heard the click of heels on the black marble floor and they saw a very smartly dressed woman walking towards them. She was wearing a black dress that flowed in the skirt like a cloud, but the bodice was tight and form fitting. Poppy could see shining black jewels glittering among the fabric making it look as if the woman was clothed in the stars themselves.

The woman had sleek red gold hair done up in an elegant updo. The jewels adorned her hair as well, so she simply sparkled. She had green eyes that shone as brightly as she did. "Poppy?"

Poppy looked at her in confusion. "Yes?"

"I'm Kaitlin! It's so wonderful to finally meet you." She gave Poppy a bright smile. "Can I give you a hug?"

Poppy smiled back. "Sure, of course you can. "

She enveloped Poppy in a soft hug. She smelled of something spicy and alluring.

"It's nice to meet you, too!" Poppy said.

"And this is the lovely Dava you told me about?" She enveloped Dava in a hug. "It's lovely to meet you! Would either of you like a drink?" Kaitlin walked back towards the bar, her heels clicking on the marble floor.

"Oh, it's not necessary," Poppy said.

"We don't want to impose. We just had some questions…" Dava said.

Love and Lemonade

Kaitlin turned and looked at both of them, her eyes widening. "Oh, but of course you're both nervous. How silly of me! Well, now we have to have a drink! Calm the nerves. I feel like a cocktail, don't you?" Kaitlin smiled and Poppy couldn't help but feel calmer.

"We don't want to take up any of your time…," Poppy said nervously.

Kaitlin smiled. "Don't be silly. This is my club and you're my patrons. We can't talk about the stuff we're going to talk about without a drink in our hands to loosen the tongue, don't you think?"

Poppy looked at Dava who nodded. They couldn't help but feel safe with Kaitlin. This was not what she thought they had been in for. Dava squeezed her hand and Poppy nodded.

"Come on, ladies. Cosmos await!" Kaitlin said

Kaitlin motioned to the bar tender. He came over quickly and bowed slightly at the table. "Yes Mistress?"

"Three cosmos please! And better bring us some munchies too. Do you ladies like calamari?"

The bar tender bowed and went back to the bar. He was soon shaking up a storm as he mixed the drinks. "Um," Poppy said. "Why did he call you Mistress?"

Kaitlin smiled. "Let's wait until we have our drinks. The night is young." She smiled when she saw Poppy's panicked look on her face. "Don't worry. I'll explain everything."

Chapter Thirty-Six

William reminded himself that there was nothing to be nervous about.

The fact that he hadn't brought a houseguest home with him since he and Mike had broken up, meant nothing. Well, no, it meant everything. David had never come here, but there had also been no one else since Michael.

He had been glad of that. In a way, Michael helped William get better. Every time he got down on himself or was being too hard on himself, William just pictured what Mike would say. Over the past few months, however, he had been taking back the condo.

Slowly, he had erased Michael's presence here. William had pulled down the wallpaper Michael had chosen, and he chose to paint in a neutral tone, and to accent the living spaces with spots of colour. It felt more like his place now, but it also seemed empty.

William hadn't realized how barren his place had felt until he watched Zack stroll around, looking at everything and taking everything in. He loved the wonder with which Zack examined everything. It was childlike, but also for some reason a bit of a turn on, watching Zack as he picked things up, ran his fingers over things and placed them back on the table or shelf.

"You strike me as a man with a killer music collection," Zack said.

"You'd be right."

"Well, where are they?" He looked around the living room and kitchen. "I don't see any."

"That's because they're in other rooms, silly."

"Rooms? As in more than one?"

William nodded. "Yep, follow me."

He took Zack's hand and there was that jolt again, the thrill that ran up his arm. He looked at Zack and wanted to kiss him, but he thought it would be better if he waited. Some things had to be savoured, after all.

William led Zack past the bathroom and into one of the bedrooms. He flicked on the light. He heard Zack gasp out loud. All along the walls, there were shelves filled with thousands of CD's and ottomans that lined the floor with his record collection. His stereo sat on a shelf beside the record player. A fifty-inch television hung on brick wall and there was another large cabinet that was filled with DVD's and BluRays.

Zack ran his fingers along the BluRays and then went to the records to flip through them. "There must be thousands of albums and movies here."

William shrugged. "I don't know. I've lost count. I do keep a catalogue of everything in my computer. Come with me, I'll show you."

He led Zack to the third bedroom and flicked on the light. Scone lights on the walls came on, glowing softly. They lit up his desk and computer and the multitude of shelves filled with hundreds and hundreds of books. Zack actually let out a sound of longing and ran to the shelves, immediately taking one down from a shelf and almost hugging it. "Oh my actual God!" he said. "Oh my God, oh my God, oh my God! How many books do you have? No, don't tell me, I want to read all of them. Have you read all of them? Which one was your favourite? No, don't tell me, I don't want to know." Zacks eyes were lit up like stars as he took in the room filled with so many books.

"Why don't you want me to tell you which book is my favourite?" William asked.

"Because people's favourite books reveal so much about them as a person, how human they are from what they love to read the most. Books reveal something internal about people, you know?"

William nodded and walked towards the shelves. Zack put the book he had been holding like a baby back on the shelf and watched William as he perused the shelves. Finally, he stopped and pulled a volume out from amongst the others and handed it to Zack.

Love and Lemonade

It was a well read, very worn, dog eared copy of The Princess Bride by William Goldman. Zack stroked the cover and William felt as if he was the one being stroked.

"The Princess Bride?" Zack said. "This is your favourite book?"

"Yes, I've read it over one hundred times. When ever I need to believe in something good, I read this book."

Zack's eyes were glassy. "I love this book. It was one of the first ones I read as a teenager. I've read it at least twice a year every year since then."

"Well, that's a relief," William said. "What's your favourite book?"

"Does it have to be just one?"

"Well, yeah. I picked one."

"Okay...I think I saw it here somewhere..." Zack searched the shelves slowly, trying to remember where he had seen the book. William loved the concentration that he saw in Zack's every movement, as if finding this book would decide the next moment between the two of them.

Zack pulled a slim book off of the shelf and handed it to William. It was a copy of Harry Potter and the Philosopher's Stone. "I wanted to pick the whole series, because it's all just really one story, you know? But since this is where everything began, it seemed only right to start at the beginning."

William looked at Zack, standing there all nervous and vulnerable and something changed within him. A fire had been lit and Zack was the match, but thankfully, the fire was just beginning and would burn nice and slow for a long time.

Still holding their books, they said nothing and fell into each other, their lips finding each other as if they hadn't drunk any water in a long time. To William's ears, it sounded like the pages themselves sighed around them.

Chapter Thirty-Seven

"What's wrong?" Mike asked, pulling Nancy closer. "You did so well tonight and the publicist told me that after you read and spoke, the books flew off the shelves."

Nancy turned to look at Mike and Mike saw the sadness there. "Babe, am I an unliveable person?"

Mike went closer to Nancy and took him in his arms. "Why would you say a thing like that?"

"My mother! She was there!"

"She was?"

"Yeah, I saw her at the edge of the crowd and she just left. She didn't even stay to say hello to me! After all this time and she didn't have anything to say! Does she hate me that much? Do I disgust her?"

Mike hugged Nancy tighter and tried to hold him together. He said nothing, but merely let Nancy breathe. He didn't cry, Nancy wasn't a crier. He was a fighter. That was one of the things that Mike loved most about him. No matter what the world threw at him, Nancy rose up to meet it head on.

He knew that Nancy was a little shaken over this, but Mike also knew that Nancy would grow from this, using the anguish that he felt in his writing. Mike was about to suggest they open a bottle of wine when there was a knock at the door of their suite.

"Who could that be?" Nancy said.

"Maybe Alyssa with more details of the next stop?"

"I don't think so. I have a couple days until we go to Toronto." Mike felt Nancy shrug. "Room service?"

"I didn't order anything yet. I was going to take you out for dinner at a fancy restaurant."

The knock came again, a little bit heavier this time. Then they heard a voice. "Are you going to make an old woman stand out here all night?"

A look of panic came over Nancy's face. "Oh my God," he said.

Mike said nothing but gently stepped away from Nancy and walked towards the door. He looked back at Nancy before he opened it. Nancy looked frightened, but determined. He would face this head on, as he had with everything else. He nodded once and Michael nodded back and opened the door.

Nancy took in a breath. There stood his mother. Instead of looking ten years older, she somehow looked just the same, as if she had paused time for both of them. He walked towards the door, reminding himself that yelling at his mother was not the way to accomplish anything.

"Hello Mom," Nancy said.

"Hello Clarence. May I come in?" She spoke with a deep voice that had always made Nancy think of Lauren Bacall.

Nancy nodded and stepped out of the way for her. His mother came in and Mike closed the door behind her.

She turned to look at Michael and take all of him in. She saw something in him that she must have approved of because she nodded and held out her hand to him. "Hello. My name is Lydia. I hope you've been taking good care of my Clarence."

Michael took her offered hand and shook it lightly. "Yes I have Ma'am. And he takes good care of me."

"I'm happy to hear that. What might your name be?"

"Michael, Ma'am."

"Michael is a fine name. And you may call me Lydia."

Lydia turned to face Nancy. She had a soft smile on her face. "Clarence. You're looking so well."

"So are you, Mama."

"I've read your book." She took What's Love Got to do With It? out of her bag. He saw that there were post it notes stuck all throughout. She used to do that when he was a kid and he had asked her why she put so many in her books. 'It's so I can remember the good bits' she had said. Her copy of his book was filled with post it notes.

"Did you like it?" Nancy asked quietly, almost as if he was afraid to hear the answer.

"Oh baby boy, I loved every word. I had no idea that you could write like this." She ran her hands over the book as if trying to keep the words within the pages.

Michael saw a tear slide from Nancy's eye. He said nothing, knowing that this was a moment between mother and son and he was merely an observer.

"I'm so glad, Mama. But if you liked it so much, why didn't you stay to see me at the store?"

"Clarence, I was there the entire time. I heard you read from your novel and it moved me. But I had to find out by seeing your book in the bookstore. I was so shocked when I saw it, the book with your name on the cover. I thought that that couldn't be my Clarence. But when I picked it up and looked at the photo on the dustjacket, there you were. My sweet baby boy."

Lydia walked closer to him. "I bought ten copies, one for me and one for each of your aunts and your sister Shelagh. She's read it too and sends her love."

"I miss her," Nancy said. "I miss you."

"Baby boy, I've been here all this time. I wanted to stay and see you, but I didn't know what to say at the time. I've been trying to think of what to say to you since I read your book. How could I sum up ten years of silence in one conversation? I couldn't. I didn't know how. Even tonight, I was wondering what I was going to say to you, what I could possibly say to make things better between us."

She placed the book down on a coffee table and held out her arms to him. "I finally decided that it doesn't matter. Time heals all wounds. I've forgiven you and I'm sorry that it's been so long. Come give mama a hug."

Love and Lemonade

Nancy looked at her as if he had been slapped. Mike had never seen him wear that particular look of shock on his face. "Forgive me?" Nancy's eyes narrowed. "Forgive *me*? Are you kidding me? *I* should be the one forgiving *you*!"

"Whatever for?" She put her arms down and put her hands on her hips. "I don't like your tone young man, not at all."

"You come in her telling me that you forgive me and you want me to watch my tone?"

"I still don't see why you're so upset," she said. "I've done nothing wrong."

Nancy snorted. "My own mother called me Nancy Boy my entire life. You told me I might as well cut my dick off if I couldn't give you children."

"So, I'm your mother, I deserve children and grand children."

"You still don't get it, do you?" he asked her.

She huffed and grabbed her book. "What I get is that you are the one who stopped talking to me. You are the one who deserves my forgiveness, not the other way around."

Lydia turned to Michael and handed him a card. "I'm staying at this hotel for a few days. You tell him to call me when he gets off his mighty high horse. It was very nice meeting you."

She looked at Nancy before slipping out of the hotel room and letting the door close behind her with a soft click.

Chapter Thirty-Eight

When they were all settled with drinks, Kaitlin raised her glass. "To new adventures," she said.

Poppy and Dava clinked glasses and they all took a sip of their cosmo. Poppy took a sip and took courage from the booze that was now running through her system. "What can you tell us about S and M?" she asked quietly.

Kaitlin smiled. "First, you don't have to whisper it like that."

"Like what?" Poppy asked.

"Like it's some dirty secret. What do you think this club is about?" She put down her drink and called out "S and M!" in a loud voice. A few of the other patrons of the club clapped and whistled. "We are in a safe place. You can both feel free to be yourselves here, okay? You don't have to hide who you are or who you want to be."

Dava shook her head. "I've had to hide who I am for most of my life."

"Well, in the S and M community, you can be free."

"I thought it was all about setting boundaries?" Poppy said.

Kaitlin nodded. "Yes, but you set your own with your partner and create a space that is totally your own and under your control. It is a space that is filled with mutual respect. There has to be trust and respect in an environment like this. We use safe words so that you are always able to stop at anytime. It's an environment of constant respect."

"What do you mean safe words? Why would you need those?" Dava asked.

Kaitlin looked as if she were deep in thought and was thinking about how best to answer. Finally, she called out. "Frederick!"

The bartender came over to the table. "Yes Mistress?"

"Is there anyone using viewing room number one?"

"No Mistress."

"We will be using it this evening. Please open the 2002 cabernet sauvignon for us and have it waiting in the room." She turned to Dava and Poppy. "Are either of you hungry?"

"We had a cookie or two before coming over," Dava said with a roguish grin.

"That's not dinner. Frederick, have a meal prepared for us. We will be eating in an hour."

"Yes Mistress."

He bowed slightly to her and walked quickly away. Dava motioned at his retreating backside with her glass. "Why does he call you Mistress?"

"It's the kind of relationship we have together. I'm his mistress and Frederick is my slave. He does what I tell him and pays me mightily for the privilege of training him."

Dava nearly choked on her glass. "I'm sorry, what?"

"Well, Masochism is all about the relationship between two people. Come ladies, walk with me." She stood and held out both of her hands, one to Poppy and one to Dava.

They each stood and looked at each other before taking the offered hand. Kaitlin walked slowly, not in a rush and content to let Poppy and Dava walk at their own paces, though their hands were joined.

"You see," Kaitlin said, "S and M is all about a relationship between a submissive and one who is dominant. Those rolls can sometimes change, but usually they don't. A submissive or a slave looks for a Master or Mistress to tell them what to do. It may be that they want the house cleaned, or that they want to lick someone's boots or be gently whipped." Kaitlin shrugged. "The relationship and its needs are set by those in the relationship. It's always consensual and always safe."

They came to a room with a heavy door covered in red velvet brocade. It was lined with gold and silver piping. Kaitlin pushed it open and they walked into what looked like a parlour filled with comfortable seats and soft lighting. Frederick stood nearby holding a bottle of wine.

"Very good Frederick. You may pour us glasses and open the viewing windows."

"Excellent Mistress."

He poured them all full glasses of wine and then pressed a button. One wall of the room seemed to slide in on itself. Dava looked at it in confusion.

"It's all right," Kaitlin said. "This is one of the viewing rooms. It's a one-way mirror and only we can see them."

The room they were looking into was lit with low lighting and filled with black furniture. There was a cross set up in the centre of the room and tied to the cross was a man. He was dressed in a black leather loincloth. There was a woman standing nearby holding a whip and she was dressed from head to toe in black leather. She approached the crucifix and began to lightly drag the whip along the man's body, tweaking his nipples with the other hand. They heard him moan in pleasure.

"Do they know that we are watching them?" Poppy said.

"My dear Poppy," Kaitlin said, smiling. "They paid handsomely for the privilege of being watched."

Chapter Thirty-Nine

The morning sun streamed through the windows and Chuck snuggled closer to Sebastian. After seeing how Sebastian had handled his daughter, Chuck was even more in love with him. Not once did Sebastian raise his voice. Instead, all he did was love Cassie.

Sebastian yawned and wrapped his arms around Chuck. "Hmmm, I love waking up with you."

"Did you ever think this would happen?" Chuck asked. "I mean you and me?"

Chuck felt Sebastian shake his head. "I didn't think there was anyone for me. I spent a lot of my life as my true self alone. I dated on and off, but never really connected to someone until I met you."

"Who wouldn't want you?" Chuck said. "I think you're beautiful."

"You have to say that because I've had your dick in my mouth."

Chuck slapped him softly. They were quiet for a bit until Chuck said, "You were alone for a long time, weren't you?"

"Yeah, I was. I didn't think I would ever find anyone that I would want to share my life with, aside from my ex-husband. I didn't think there was anyone who would love me for me, the true me, until I met you."

Chuck put his hand along Sebastian's chest and rested his hand right above Sebastian's heart. Chuck listened to the heartbeat through the touch of his fingers. "I love you."

"I love you too."

They kissed and Chuck was still surprised by the electricity that ran through him when his lips met Sebastian's. It was the same every time and never failed to take his breath away. Chuck felt the stirrings of something down below, but he pushed those thoughts aside so that he could say what he had to say.

It had been bothering him and bothering him and he had to say something. Chuck had to let Sebastian know what he'd done.

"Babe..."

Sebastian snuggled closer. "Yeah?"

"I have something that I should tell you."

At that moment, however, the words stuck in Chuck's mouth as the bedroom door slammed open. Cassandra was standing there looking at Chuck as if he were the devil's playmate and he must be vanquished.

"You fucking asshole."

"Cassie, I can-"

"You don't get to speak!" She said.

"What's going on here?" Sebastian had pulled the covers up to cover his chest in front of his daughter.

"You fucking cocksucking ass fucking asshole!"

"Well, I may be all of those things, but-" Chuck said.

"Cassie! Your language!" Sebastian said.

"Fuck my language! And fuck him, that's what you were about to do, so I'll let you get on with it for fuck's sake. Fuck fuck fuckety fuck!"

She turned to go when Sebastian spoke up. "Cassie! What's the matter? What happened?"

When she turned around, they saw that the fire had died in her and was now replaced with an ocean of sadness. "What happened? This fucker," she pointed at Chuck, "Called Geoff's mom and told her I'm pregnant. Fucking fucker asshole buttmunch."

Without another word, she stalked out of the bedroom, leaving Sebastian looking at Chuck in shock.

Chapter Forty

"So, here's the thing…," Curtis said. "I have something to tell you, but I'm not sure how you're going to take it."

They were walking in the park across from Curtis' apartment. Devon's hand was warm and Curtis relished the feel of it.

"Sure, sexy," Devon said. "It can't be any worse than finding out you were a drag queen, so I think you're good."

"Well, no, it's not that, it's more important than being a drag queen, not that that's important or anything, but well, that is kind of important, but not as important as this. So…yeah."

Devon smiled and kissed Curtis softly on the lips. "Gee, thanks for clearing that up. You made things a lot easier to understand."

"Oh, god, I'm sorry! I'm making a mess of this."

"Hey, it's okay." Devon gave Curtis' hands a squeeze and then kissed them. "Whatever it is, we'll handle it. It can't be all that bad can it?" He leaned in and kissed him again. "And never apologize, baby. You are who you are."

"Okay. Okay, okay." He took a deep breath and then he looked at Devon, at his gorgeous brown eyes that he could fall into and find himself somewhere in Devon's soul.

Somehow, looking into Devon's eyes brought him calmness even though what he was about to say frightened him so very much.

"Here's the thing. I've never really loved any guy that I've been with. Sure, I liked them fine and I had relationships with a few men, but nothing that went very far. I always thought that they wanted me to be something different than I was. Quite often that was the truth, no matter how I wished it not to be so."

"What are you saying, Curtis?"

"Let me finish, please. I've had these words in my head for weeks and they need to get out. I don't know if I can hold on to them any longer. The thing is that none of those men were you. When you look at me, you see the real me, the whole me and you haven't once asked me to change who I am despite being a drag queen and a bit neurotic."

"Baby, you don't have to change anything. I may not understand the drag queen thing, but I'll try to wrap my head around it if you will take the time to teach me all about it. But that's not what's bothering you right now is it?"

Curtis took a deep breath. "Well, I've never said these words before, and this may come as a shock to you, but..." Curtis looked into Devon's brown eyes and saw a twinkle there. It inspired him to keep going. "But I love you. I think I've loved you since I saw you back in the days where you used to prowl the bars looking for guys and I just prayed that you would look at me. But I don't just love you for your body.

Love and Lemonade

I love all of you, every scar, every hair, every crease of skin. I love everything about you, I love your laugh, your sense of humour, the way you care about other people."

Taking another deep breath, Curtis looked away for a second, trying to gather himself and then looked back at Devon. *Gods, how did he get even more gorgeous every time he looked at him?* "The thing is: I love you. That's all I wanted to say."

Curtis looked away again, not willing to see Devon's face as it broke open in a mocking smile or a sneer. Curtis was sure that Devon would be a person who would use a sneer when telling someone off or laughing at them and he would probably look so fucking hot doing it, too. Then he felt his face being pulled gently back again.

"Hey," Devon said. "Is it very loud in there?"

"What do you mean?"

"You look like you're thinking a million and one thoughts."

Curtis shrugged. "Yeah. I tend to do that. It's the drama queen in me."

"Well, stop. I have something to say to you, too."

"Okay." Curtis tried to calm his breathing.

"I've been trying to think of a way to tell you for weeks now and you took the words right out of my mouth. I love the way you can move across the room as if you own it, I love how your loyal to your friends and loved ones and put them first, I love how confident you are, getting up on stage and being someone completely different, but still somehow lovely and so very you."

"Okay." Curtis had to remind himself to breathe. He had never received so many compliments all at one time.

"I love everything about you. I love how you look, the way you kiss thrills me, and I love the silhouette of your body through the shower curtain in the morning when you're taking a shower. I love everything about you because I love you. I love you, Curtis."

"I love you, Devon."

When they kissed, this time, Curtis thought it felt different, as if the kiss resounded through his whole body somehow. So, he deepened the kiss with Devon, to see if he could somehow hold on to this feeling, so he could know it and never let it go.

When the kiss ended, and they pulled away, Curtis saw that the sparkle in Devon's eyes had intensified. "God, you are so cute."

"Why?"

"Where do I start?" Devon asked. "Have you really wanted to tell me for weeks?"

"Yep."

"Well, next time, when you want to say something to me, just say it, okay?"

"No matter what it is?"

"No matter what," Devon said.

Love and Lemonade

"Okay. I need a male model for my next drag number and I've decided that it has to be you."

Devon let out a gasp. "What?"

"Well, now that we love each other, you can't have me macking on another guy, can you?" Curtis said with a grin.

Chapter Forty-One

Dillon hadn't expected to find a Josephine Daniels in the phone book. When he looked up the name, he saw that there was only one name listed. On an impulse, and before he lost his nerve, he called the number.

An older woman answered the phone. "Yes?"

"Is this Ms. Josephine Daniels?"

"It's Mrs. Daniels. But yes, this is she. Who is calling please?"

"My name is Dillon Majors. I'm calling about your niece Rebecca Daniels?"

There was the sound of a gasp taken in. "Oh, gracious. I haven't heard her name in years. And who are you?"

"I'm the man who is in love with her and hopes to marry her some day."

"Then why the hell are you calling me?"

Dillon could tell from listening to Josephine's voice that this woman would appreciate honesty and being forthright. He also knew that she would be able to call bullshit should he speak any and he would lose his chance to find out more of what happened to Rebecca.

"Well, it was something that she said the other day to me. She said that her friends and family had cut her off and she had no need of them. That sounded so sad to me. It was also the first time she had mentioned her family to me. I had assumed that she had been an only child and had lost her parents. I had no idea that any of her family were alive."

"Then why are you calling me?"

"My brother, Devon, is her best friend. He said he remembered Rebecca saying something about you."

"You're Devon's brother?"

"You met him?"

"Yes, probably ten years ago now. Tell me, are you not hard on the eyes either? Devon was a looker."

Dillon let out a small chuckle. "Well, I do hope Rebecca thinks so."

"She was always a good judge of character, our Rebecca. All except for that one time."

Suddenly a light bulb went off inside of Dillon's head. He remembered the conversation they had had so long ago: *Love never dies. It just takes on a different form when someone is gone from our lives, whether it be from reaching their end, or another reason.*

"Did that one time have anything to do with Jackson and Samantha?" Dillon asked.

"If you mean that rat bastard and the baby she almost had, then yes. It has everything to do with them." He heard her take in a breath. "You have done your homework, haven't you?"

Dillon simply said "I love her. I want her to be my wife. But I want her to be happy more than anything."

"Even more than your own happiness?"

"She's what makes me happy. I've never known anyone like her. I want to continue loving her, but I want her to happy so much."

Josephine let out a laugh that sounded like the tinkle of bells. "Oh, she has reeled you in. Very well, I think that perhaps we should meet. Are you free tomorrow for a luncheon? I'm partial to a good smoked meat sandwich and a bowl of soup. Talia's makes a lovely one and I can meet you there."

"I'd love that, Mrs. Daniels."

"Oh, please call me Jo. Mrs. Daniels sounds like my mother."

Chapter Forty-Two

Romilda had been trying to get a hold of Eldecot Johnsen for a while now. He wasn't answering her phone calls or her messages. She knew he only wanted one thing so, with a big sigh, she went into his office and sat down for a good long wait.

She had just taken out her knitting and was knitting one, purling two when she heard the click of expensive dress shoes on the shiny marble floors. A young woman with sleek red hair done in an elegant updo and a kind face approached her.

"Miss Robinson? I'm Alex, Eldecot's assistant. He's ready to see you now."

"Well, he can just wait until I'm finished this row."

Alex stood there watching her for a moment. Then she asked: "What is it you're knitting?"

"As if you care." Romilda reminded herself that this woman had done nothing wrong. She sighed. "Sorry dear, I've got my morning bitch face on," Romilda said. "It's not you, it's the horrid lack of caffeine in my system."

"Oh, what are you knitting?" Alex asked.

"A sweater for my beau. It's cold out and he never dresses sensibly."

"Pfft, like all men!" Alex gave her a bright smile. "What kind of yarn are you using?"

"Lambswool, so that way it won't be itchy."

"Good choice, and I love the colour! That deep purple will be lovely."

"Yes, and it will bring out the colour in his eyes," Romilda said.

As she finished the row, she marvelled at the oddness of fate. Who would have thought she would meet a potential friend while coming to meet an enemy? She put her yarn and knitting needles away thinking that fate was strange like that.

"Okay, Alex, lead me to the prick now," Romilda said with a wry grin.

Alex snorted. "Right this way, please."

As they walked down a hallway made from white marble, Alex said, "You know, I belong to a knitting group. We get together and have a good knit and natter every week or so. Let me know if you'd like to pop by sometime."

Despite herself, Romilda was touched. "I'd like that, thank you."

Alex nodded and knocked softly on a door marked E. Johnsen. A voice said "Enter!" from behind the door. Alex gave Romilda another kind smile and opened the door for her.

"A Miss. Robinson to see you, sir."

"Ah, yes. Thank you, Miss Brown. Please see that we're not disturbed."

"Yes, sir."

Alex closed the door behind her, leaving Romilda and Eldecot alone together. He motioned at a leather chair. "Please, have a seat," he said.

"No, I don't think I will."

He sighed. "Really, Romilda? Do we have to do it this way?"

"Yes, we do."

"We used to be…friends once upon a time. Are you sure that I can't interest you in a beverage? Some nice red, perhaps. I think I have a bottle of your favourite on hand."

She gave him a wide grin. "Well, why didn't you say so."

Eldecot smiled and went to a small bar that he had in the corner of his office. He brought the bottle and two glasses and placed them on the coffee table. "Please, sit."

"No, I don't think I will."

Eldecot's smile faded. "I thought we were going to have a nice drink of wine and talk like friends."

"Funny, we weren't friends, we were lovers."

"Yes, but to be lovers, we had to be friends, first."

"You were never my friend. You just looked at me like a possession. It just took me too long to see it."

"Come now, we had fun, didn't we?"

"Yeah, we did, until I found out about the other ladies you kept on the side."

He actually laughed. "You still think you alone could have satisfied me?"

"We'll never know, will we?" Romilda glared at him and tried to communicate the dislike she felt for him in that gaze. "So why are you threatening to close the library? Why can't you leave me alone and let me be?"

"Well, it's simple, really. You were the one who got away."

"What? What the hell are you talking about?"

"You're the only woman I dated who left me."

"That can't be all of it. You really can't be that simple."

"I can be and I will be," Eldecot said with glee, not realizing that Romilda had just called him stupid and simple minded. "You left me before I was done with you. Now it's time for me to collect."

"You can't be fucking serious!" Romilda spluttered.

"Yes, I am. Come back to me, or the library building will be demolished in a few months. You're mine, Romilda. Don't you forget it."

"We'll fucking see about this." She stalked towards the door and stopped, doubled back and grabbed the unopened bottle of wine.

"Where are you going with that?" Eldecot asked. "That's a three-hundred dollar bottle of wine!"

"Well, what's mine is yours, right? Fucker." Putting the bottle of wine in her bag, she left the office, slamming the door behind her.

Chapter Forty-Three

"I don't understand why you're freaking out." Connie said.

They were at Talia's and the waitress brought her a margarita and brought William a coffee. He gave her a sardonic look.

"What?" she said. "It's nearly lunchtime. Plus, margaritas have protein."

"Where, exactly?"

"In the fucking lime juice. Anyway, what does it matter? We ordered food. And I came here because you called me. What's the problem?"

"Gosh, aren't you a ray of fucking sunshine."

"Spare me. You're getting laid at least. I've been in a months long dry spell."

"So go out and meet someone, why don't you?"

"Can't. Everyone knows who I am and I've gotten the reputation of an angry lawyer, thanks to Poppy."

"That was kind of your fault. Why don't you just try to go out and meet someone?" William asked. "I mean, I met Zack without even trying."

"Yeah, well I'm a lost cause, so back to you. Why are we here, aside from the wonderful margaritas?"

"Well, Zack stayed over last night."

"Oh, give me the juicy and naughty details!" Connie said.

"He's so lovely. I gave him a tour of my place."

"I'm sure you did. Did you show him the sling you keep in the bedroom and the mirror on the ceiling?"

"Don't be crass."

"Why not? You fucking love it."

"True, but I'm trying to tell you about my romantic date."

"Oh God, you're talking about romance already."

"Well, yeah. It was very romantic. He was so awed by everything, but most of all the library."

Connie took a sip of her margarita. "I do have to admit it, your library even makes me wet."

"I know, right? But you should have seen his face. It was like he was a kid in the most amazing candy store there was. And the way he kissed me afterwards! I've never met anyone so turned on by books!"

"So how was the old rumple foreskin? Spare me the intricate details on that, please. I don't want to barf into my drink."

"We didn't have sex."

Connie blinked at him and took another sip of her drink. "I'm sorry honey, I must be more drunk than I thought. It sounds like you said you and Zack didn't even have sex."

"We didn't."

"Well then what the fuck did you do?"

Love and Lemonade

"We made out for a while and I know that we both got hard, but it as like we both knew that there was no need to rush things, that we had time, so we could take our time and enjoy each other. He told me a lot about growing up and about his family. I told him about mine. It was so wonderful. We're already getting together again tonight."

Connie blinked at him again and took yet another sip of her drink. "Listen to yourself. Do you hear yourself at all?"

"Sure, I do. I'm happy. Zack makes me deliriously happy."

Connie snorted. "Toots, you're not just happy. You're in love." She lit a cigarette and blew out smoke rings.

William didn't know what to say, so he said nothing but there was such a large smile on his face that anyone seeing it would be put into a good mood. "In love…," he said finally. He looked positively, deliriously happy.

Connie let out a loud snort and ordered another margarita.

Chapter Forty-Four

Blaine still couldn't believe it.

He had put all the paintings together for Remmy Pecora for his own exhibition. There were thirty paintings, almost all of them portraits of people he knew or people he had met. Some of them he loved or had loved, some of them he had seen only in passing, others he had known for an afternoon.

All of the people in these paintings spoke to him in some way. Some of them had never spoken to him in reality, so instead they would speak to him this way, in his creations. It was also his way of preserving a bit of time, a single moment, a piece of thought of circumstance. In this way, he could stop time, albeit temporarily. Blaine wondered if it as in a way his super power.

Blaine had always viewed art this way. It was his way of writing like Nancy did, except he'd dance across a canvass instead of a page. Every canvas he did told a story, some of them happier than others. Looking at the thirty paintings that he had assembled to make up his exhibition, he wondered what story he was trying to tell by assembling them all together.

Blaine stood and looked at all the canvases while Justin stood beside him and Remmy walked along and examined each one. She stood in front of some more than others, and with others still even longer.

Justin squeezed his hand. "Breathe, Babe."

"I am breathing," Blaine said.

"Breathe deeply then. You're so tightly wound."

"No, I'm not."

"Yes, you are. You're crushing my fingers."

"Oh!" Blaine let go of Justin's hand so that Justin could wiggle his fingers to get life back into them. "I'm sorry. I'm a little nervous."

"It's okay, Babe. I got your back."

"You know," Remmy said, "It's awfully hard for someone to focus when others are whispering." She turned smiling. "Or didn't teachers at school teach you that."

"They did," Blaine said. "But I never listened anyway."

Remmy let out a loud laugh. "I like you Blaine. You've got bucketloads of talent and you have a sense of humour. A lot of artists I know are too serious for themselves, always going on about inspirations and education. Tell me, have you ever taken a course? Do you follow a lot of artists? Do you like to imitate what you see?"

He thought about it for a moment. "No, I've never taken an art course. I just learn from doing and I've gotten better over time. I don't follow a lot of different artists because I don't want them to influence what I do and I have enough trouble doing what I do; why would I want to imitate art by other people?"

"Spoken like a true artist. So, all of this is self-taught?" She gestured at the paintings and strolled along to look at them again.

"Yes, Ma'am," Blaine said.

Remmy let out a sigh. "I've told you before not to call me that. It makes me feel old." She turned to Justin. "Do you know how talented your partner is?"

"I do."

"Does he have any idea how talented he is?"

Justin gave Blaine a look filled with love. "I don't think he did when we met, but he's beginning to have some idea."

"Good, that's good." She went up to Blaine and hugged him softly. "You are going to make a shitload of money."

"Does that mean you think the paintings are good?"

She turned to Justin again. "I thought you said that he was beginning to understand how amazing he is?"

Justin shrugged. "Meh, he's a work in progress."

Remmy turned back to Blaine. "Do you have any good you are? Your grasp of light and shadow, your use of form…Your work leaves me speechless. Have you ever had an exhibition before?"

"No, I give them as gifts to friends. I really just paint for myself."

"Well, I can promise you that all that will change after next week. You capture these people better than a photo could." Remmy had a flush in her cheeks that made her look more beautiful than she already was. "I can't wait to have your show. I've booked some reporters to come and talk to you, just people from the leading art magazines. Tell me, what kind of paint do you use?"

"A mixture of acrylic and oil, depending on the look for the piece that I want." He scratched his head. "Do you really think they're that good?"

"Blaine, they are amazing. I haven't seen eyes so real since I studied Klimt when I was in art history school. I was always drawn towards art; I just had no talent for it. Thankfully, I recognize it in others." She placed a hand on his shoulder. "I can't wait for your exhibition. You will have to come up with a title for it."

"A title?"

"Yes. You're telling a story, aren't you? What will you call that story?"

Blaine didn't have to think about it. "People I have known."

Remmy smiled. "Simple, poetic. Lovely. I'm so excited for you. I can't wait until your show. I just know it will be a hit!"

Blaine smiled back, but he couldn't shake the feeling that he was living in a dream and that this was somehow all going to come to a crashing end.

Chapter Forty-Five

Cordellia tried to tell herself that everything would be all right. The truth was that she knew it wouldn't be, not ever again.

Her whole world was falling apart. Joe was the best thing to happen to her life and the only man she had ever loved. She had loved Romilda in her previous life, but not like she had loved Joe. She loved Joe with everything she had, every breath and every fibre of her being; and right now, every piece of her was hurting.

That was nothing to how Joe felt, she knew. Still, though, there must be something she could do to ease his heart. She thought she had an idea. Cordellia hoped it was a good idea. Blaine and Justin had said they would come and a few of the others had agreed as well and she hoped they would show.

She marched into the living room where Joe was sitting and reading a book, but she could tell that he wasn't really reading the words. He hadn't turned a page in over an hour. "All right, let's get going. Is that what you're wearing?"

Joe looked up from the book confused. "I'm sorry? Cordy, what are you talking about?"

"I'm talking about going out and getting you shit faced, that's what!"

Love and Lemonade

"Honey, it's not even noon."

"So, it's beer o'clock somewhere and the bars open at eleven. Come on, get up, get dressed, we're going out."

"I don't really feel like going out, love."

"It's because of that that I'm taking you out. We can't sit here like a bunch of sad sacks feeling sorry for ourselves. We have a wedding to plan and if we're going to do it in under a week, we need help."

"What are you talking about? We can't get married in a week."

"We can and we will. I've waited thirty years to be your wife and not even you having cancer will stop me." She stood in front of Joe with her hands on her hips. "Now, you get your ass moving so we can go. We have to be there in ten minutes."

"Where are we going?"

"Well, I was thinking of a fancy place, but I suppose The Cabin will do. It's always been the place where the boys hang out and where we all feel most comfortable. It seemed right, to plan a wedding there, don't you think?"

"Love, I don't think-" Joe began.

"You don't have to think. Go put on those jeans that are ripped slightly in the back pocket. I love looking at your ass in those."

He gave her a grin. "I don't suppose I'm getting out of this, huh?"

"You suppose right. Now get a move on."

She watched him leave and there was a bounce in his step. She was glad. He had been so down and so withdrawn for weeks. He had not been the man that she had fallen in love with, but instead, had been a shadow of himself.

Cordellia desperately hoped that everything would go to plan. Although, she was doing everything without a plan, so who knew what would happen. All she knew was that he deserved happiness and she was going to give it to him.

And she would take a little for herself along the way, too.

Chapter Forty-Six

Nancy knew that Michael was worried about him. Seeing his mother had shaken him up, had shaken up his whole world.

Hell, meeting Nancy's mother had shaken up Michael's whole world. It wasn't that it redefined what he thought of Nancy, only that there was so much that he still didn't know about Nancy. Michael couldn't wait to learn all that he could about him.

After Lydia had left, Michael had taken Nancy out to dinner. Along the way, they had stopped at a vendor's market that was open. Michael had watched Nancy trail his fingers over all the shiny things while looking at them with longing.

"Pick something you want, Babe. It's on me."

Nancy turned and gave him a stern look. "I will not let you buy me a pity gift because my mothers a ninny."

"I'm buying it for you because I'm proud of you and what you did tonight."

"Oh, in that case, I'll take that necklace and this ring and possibly those earrings."

"You're going to sparkle!"

"Honey, I already sparkle. This will just intensify the effect!"

The vendor had bagged up Nancy's purchases and they had a lovely dinner in downtown Montreal. While they ate pizza and had a few glasses of wine, the lights from the street as well as the noises of people and cars outside the window, were kind of like music.

Very softly, Michael said, "Tell me what happened."

Nancy put down his piece of pizza and picked up his glass of wine. "There's not much to tell, really." Nancy shrugged. "I was born in a middle-class family. There was nothing special about it, I didn't live in a hood or anything. My parents loved me and they loved each other very much."

"So, what happened?" Michael asked.

"My mom knew that I was gay before I did. She was always calling me Nancy Boy, with a smile. Over time, I thought it was just our little joke, that it was something to laugh about. I started asking to be called Nancy, not Clarence. My family agreed, even my sisters started calling me Nancy. It was the first time that I felt at home with my name, you know?"

Michael nodded and took Nancy's hand and gave it a squeeze. He let the silence stretch on because he wanted Nancy to be comfortable enough to continue. He hadn't talked about any of this in all the time that Michael had known him. Michael knew that the words would have to come out slowly.

"It was when I finally realized what I was, that I was gay. I started reading anything I could to learn about who I was, whether there were others like me. I had never slept with a man at that point, but I knew what I was. I knew who I was. I started to experiment with how I dressed and with wearing eye shadow."

A look of pain crossed Nancy's face, covering it in a mask that Michael didn't recognize for Nancy had not worn pain on his face for as long as Michael had known him. He had only known Nancy to wear a look of joy on his face, or one of fierceness or anger. He had never seen him look sad once in all the years he had known him, and it pained Michael to no end. He wanted to take Nancy into his arms right then, but he knew that Nancy had to get this out, he had to say those words that he had kept buried in the dark for so long.

"When the kids at school saw me wearing nail polish and eye shadow, they started calling me faggot. They would write it on my locker and tease me. I didn't care. It wasn't until one of them started to taunt me, calling me Nancy Boy that I snapped. I ended up getting into a fight with that boy, the one that used my moms special name for me. I was sent home and suspended for a week. When my mom picked me up and drove me home, she asked me what happened. So, I told her."

Nancy let out sigh, as if the memory itself pained him. "She said that I was wrong to beat up the other boy. That I was a Nancy Boy and why not just admit it, so the secrecy could end. If I was going to be an embarrassment, I could at least own up to it."

Nancy's voice had taken on a dead tone, as if repeating all the words were taking something from him, some of the joy that he carried with him like a flame against the dark. "It was never the same between my mom and me after that. After I realized that she had been making fun of me, mocking me for years and right in front of my face, with the family in on the joke. I barely spoke to my mom after that, only when I absolutely had to. I still loved her, she was my mom, but I saw her for what she was, you know?"

Nancy looked up at Michael and, although Nancy wasn't crying, the pain was laid bare for Michael to see. "I left home when I was young. A bunch of drag queens took me in. They never understood why I never tried on a dress, but they loved what I could do with make up."

Michael smiled. There was that little bit of light that shone, despite the shadow that swirled around in his eyes. He loved Nancy more than ever right then and Michael knew that he could do whatever was necessary to make sure Nancy knew that he was loved.

They strolled hand in hand back to the hotel room. "Are you excited to be going on to Toronto?" Michael asked.

"Yeah, I can't wait. I think I'm done with Montreal for a while."

They turned the corner and standing in front of their hotel room was Lydia, Nancy's mom.

Nancy stopped walking and stared with open dislike written all over his face. "What are you doing here?"

"Don't I have any right to be where I please?" she said.

Nancy crossed his arms in front of his chest. "Suppose you don't."

Lydia's eyes widened, and she wagged her finger at Nancy. "Oh no, you don't get to play that card with me, mister. I don't care what happened between us, I am still your mother and you are still my son. Don't you dare challenge me because you will lose!"

There was silence as Nancy and Lydia looked at each other, their chests heaving with heavy breaths and things left unsaid.

"Wow," Michael said.

Nancy turned to look at him. He had almost forgotten Michael was even there; he had been focusing on his mother so much.

"Wow? Wow what?"

"Now I know where you get your look from."

"What look?" Nancy asked.

"That look you get when someone pisses you off and your about to bust a cap in their ass." He nodded to Lydia. "No offense Ma'am."

"None taken." Lydia said.

"You know the look," Michael continued. "The look when you're about to lose it or you're about to give us a sermon on why we're wrong about something."

"Because you usually are wrong about something!" Nancy shrieked.

"I see you haven't changed much," Lydia said. She smiled and approached them both. She held out her arms wide and the smile softened. "Who wants a hug?"

"No thank you," Nancy said.

"Now don't be like that. Come here and see Mama."

She enveloped him in her arms and pulled him close. Michael watched as Nancy visibly relaxed and snuggled closer to his mom. He didn't think he had ever seen him so relaxed, except when he slept.

Lydia pulled away from the hug. "Now it's your turn," she said to Michael.

Michael held up both of his hands. "It's okay, really."

"Okay nothing, you come here and give me a hug."

Michael shuffled closer and let himself be hugged by Lydia. He was surprised by how wonderful it felt being hugged by a mother. He couldn't remember the last time he had been hugged by his mother like this.

"Um, Mom?" Nancy said.

"Yes dear."

"Why is there a suitcase by our hotel room door?"

"Oh, because I'm coming with you on your book tour, honey!"

Michael saw that Nancy now had another look on his face, but it wasn't one of defiance. It was one of total horror.

Then Nancy's phone rang.

Chapter Forty-Seven

Cassandra still wasn't talking to him. Chuck wasn't surprised. If someone had pulled what he had done on him, Chuck would have busted a cap in their ass. However, for that to happen, Chuck would have to be pregnant and he found the very idea frightening, so it was probably best to leave that there.

They were getting dressed in their fancy duds. Cordellia said to meet them at the GLBT Library. Blaine and Justin were there decorating with Romilda's help and the staff at Talia's were catering the whole thing for free. They were bringing over the food now.

Standing in the doorway to Cassandra's bedroom, Chuck watched as she fluffed her hair. She didn't need to fluff it; her curls were natural and had lots of body. He sighed. "Honey, your hair is fine. Your dress if fine too, you look beautiful."

"I'll fucking tell you when I'm beautiful, you asshole. You don't get to tell me that, you don't get to speak for me when you should have remained *silent!*" She hissed the last word. She had been doing a lot of hissing around him lately."

Chuck moved further into the room. "Cassie, I'm sorry. I'm very sorry. I truly am. I took something from you when I told Chuck's mother."

Cassandra snorted. "What did you take from me?"

"Your power. I took your choice from you. I took your voice from you. I took your voice."

Cassandra stopped fussing with her hair and stared at him wide eyed in the mirror. "Yeah," she said in a small voice. "Yeah, you did."

"I'm sorry. I'm truly sorry for that. But if there are going to be decisions made about this baby, you and Geoff will have to do it together. You made the baby together, you should both decide what to do."

"Why is it so important to you that I talk to fuckwit fart face?"

Chuck thought about how to say this part. He knew why it was important that the father of Cassie's baby be involved, but no one else did. "I never knew my father," he said softly.

Cassie's eyes widened in shock. "Like, ever?"

Shaking his head, Chuck said, "Nope. He left my mother when he found out she was pregnant. She tried to find him when I started asking questions, but eventually she had to tell me the truth. I started looking at every man who kind of looked like me and wondered if that man was my father." He paused. "I suppose I called because I didn't want your kid not knowing his father, whatever happens, you know?"

They shared a beat of silence between them, but this one was different from the silence that had been between them before. The old silence was filled with so many words, screamed at him in silence. Now, the silence was filled with no words but a shifting of emotions.

"I'm sorry," Cassie said.

"Why are you sorry? I was the one who behaved like an asshat."

"Oh no, I think I own the asshat title for sure." Cassie replied, holding up a finger. "I've been all cunty to you lately."

"With good reason."

"How about Geoff wears the ass hat and you both agree to kiss and make up?" A voice said from behind Chuck. Sebastian was standing there, a soft smile on his face and he was dressed in one of his suits that made him look even more handsome in Chuck's eyes.

"That sounds good to me," Chuck said. "How about you Cassie?"

"Well, what will I say to Geoff and his mother when they come?"

"You just have to speak from your heart. And we'll be right beside you, okay honey?" Sebastian told her.

"Okay." Cassie looked at Chuck with a smile on her face and a mischievous twinkle in her eyes. "Fuckwit," she said softly.

Chapter Forty-Eight

Sasha eyed Curtis with eyes filled with wanting. "Oh Babycakes, you have never looked more gorgeous!"

Curtis did a curtsy. "You say that to all the drag queens."

"No, honey, only you. Carlotta Men has a real glow about her. You look like you're floating when you move around."

"I got myself a new girdle. It's not as tight as the bone one or using duct tape, and it lets me actually breathe. Going to the loo is a bit of a bitch, but one must suffer for beauty, mustn't they?"

Letting out a laugh, Sasha smacked Curtis' bottom. "You silly bitch. No, there's something different about you. You're different."

Curtis blushed. "I feel different."

"I know that blush," Sasha said.

"No, you don't."

"Yes, I do. You blushed like that back when we used to watch Labyrinth before you came out and you always used to stare at David Bowie's junk."

"I have no idea what you're insinuating."

"I'm not insinuating nothing, bitch."

"Well then just tell me what you mean, because I have no idea!" Curtis said, throwing up his hands.

"You love him," Sasha said.

"Yeah." He looked like a happy kid in a candy store.

"No, I mean, you *love* him. Like body and soul and all that glittery shit."

He looked at her. "Yeah, I do."

"And he loves you back? Does he even love Carlotta?"

"Well, he only recently met her, but I think he'll come to love her."

"Thankfully you're not a complete and total bitch when you're in drag, like the rest of those fucking bitches."

"There is that," Curtis said.

"Well, I'm happy you're in love Babycakes. But he and I have to have some words together."

"Sasha, you don't need to."

"I know I don't need to; you can take care of your own. I want to. It's just one of the services I offer as your bet fag hag."

There was the sound of footsteps and Devon came into the room. He smiled brightly when he saw Curtis and went over to him. He kissed Curtis' forehead.

"What? Don't want to kiss him in drag?" Sasha said.

Devon shrugged. "Doesn't bother me. I just don't want to mess up his makeup."

"Oh." Sasha raised an eyebrow. "Okay than. But I have something to tell you, Mr. Tall Dark and Handsome."

"You think I'm handsome? Thanks." Devon grinned at Curtis.

Sasha raised an eyebrow and he quieted. "You hurt him in any way, mind me when I say any way whatsoever, I will pull your balls out of your asshole and use your testicles as a punching bag."

Devon blanched. "My, that was unnecessarily graphic."

"Are we clear?"

"Crystal," Devon said, taking hold of one of Curtis' hands and pulling him close for a soft kiss, right on the lips.

As Curtis performed as Carlotta, Devon couldn't help but appreciate how he moved. He had seen a lot or drag queens over the years, especially in the clubs where he had prowled to find his next fuck. The majority of them walked like truckers, plowing across the stage with neither the grace or the beauty of a real woman.

When Devon had asked one of them why they walked like that, the drag queen had replied: "Well, this is how women walk, ain't it?"

Curtis, however, didn't merely walk across the stage. He glided across it. It didn't even look as if he was walking. As Devon watched Curtis, he was reminded of the flow of birds or the path of stars. Devon couldn't believe that Curtis could walk that way in high heels.

He rubbed his pocket and the little velvet box that hid inside. He wondered if it would be weird giving him a ring while he was dressed as a woman? And how could he strut around that stage with such confidence, but lack some of that confidence when the high heels came off?

Devon wondered if he could somehow show Curtis what he meant to him. He hoped that what lay within the little velvet box would go a little way toward showing Curtis that.

Curtis performed three numbers that night: "Diamonds are a Girls Best Friend" and "These Boots Were Made for Walking" which were numbers that he had heard before but never before had he seen them preformed with such ease and panache. Curtis as Carlotta, really was a comedian.

The third number made Curtis sit up a little straighter. Gone were the theatrics, the grand gestures, the comedic routine. Instead, there was a simple spotlight and Curtis as Carlotta sang a song that Dolly Parton had done but Whitney had made famous. Devon was glad Curtis had chosen the Dolly Parton version for it had always been his favourite.

When the opening notes of the song started to play, he sat up so that he could lean in to look closely at Curtis. He needn't have bothered. Curtis as Carlotta walked down off the stage and walked right to him and Sasha at their table. Carlotta sang 'I Will Always Love You' right to him. Devon didn't know when he had loved someone so much.

He thought of Nancy for a millisecond and dismissed him. In the end, what he had felt for Nancy had been only a very strong lust. With Curtis, he wanted to know everything about him, everything that made him tick, everything he loved. He hoped he would get the chance to after tonight.

Devon waited until the song had finished and he wiped the tears from his eyes, took the box from the pocket of his pants and kneeled on the ground.

Curtis looked confused. "What are you doing?"

"Something that feels right. The only right thing I've ever done." He opened the box to reveal the silver band that lay within and the diamond that was embedded in its surface. "Curtis, will you be mine?"

"What do you mean?" His voice shook with emotion.

"This is a promise ring. I promise to love you, to stand by you, to never hurt you and to give you half my heart. I know its old fashioned, but I wanted you to know how I felt about you. Will you accept me?"

Devon held his breath, sure that Curtis would say no, that he would end this night alone, that Curtis would walk away from him.

Instead, with tears sliding down his cheeks and his mouth wearing a huge, happy smile, Curtis said, "Yes, Devon. Yes!"

As Curtis hugged him, Devon thought once again of Nancy and how he had told Devon not to let love slip by him if it came by again. Devon hoped that he had done Nancy proud tonight and he hugged Curtis a little closer.

Chapter Forty-Nine

Zack looked amazing. He was wearing a silver blazer with jeans. The silver made his hair an even more vibrant red.

"Do you think your friends will mind me coming along? They don't know me or anything, so I kind of feel like I'll be crashing the party."

William kissed him softly. "You're my date. Besides, I like you a lot, so that ought to count for something, right?"

"It's…Okay. I think…you're won…derful."

William gave Zack a concerned look. "Zack, are you okay?" His speech had been fine one moment and slow the next. William hoped that it wasn't anything to worry about.

Zack shook his head and swallowed a few times. He took a few deep breaths. "Sorry, I'm sorry."

William went to him. "Why are you sorry?"

"I'm a little nervous. I should have told you. When I get stressed or nervous, my symptoms come to the surface."

"Which ones? Maybe if we know which ones, we can do something to battle them."

Zack turned into William's embrace. "That's kind of you to say, but it's impossible to know which ones will come to the surface. Or if all of them will."

"What kind of symptoms?"

"Well, where to start?" He looked upward as if trying to wrack his brain into proper thought. "Brain fog, fatigue, speech difficulties, vertigo, balance issues, numbness, difficulty walking. I brought my cane, just in case. I never know how they will show themselves. Whenever they come back, they are always slightly different."

"What do you mean they're different?"

"It's always different each time. That's why relapse and remitting MS is so difficult to deal with. There's no telling what it will do."

William wanted to pull Zack into another embrace. He looked so fragile right now. But William knew that there was a core of strength to him, that Zack was stronger than he thought he was.

"Tell me about what just happened. When you had difficulty speaking."

"You don't want to hear about this." Zack waved a hand in the air.

"You're wrong. I do. I want to know all of you and this is part of you. So, what's it like? I can't begin to imagine what you go through so you'll have to tell me."

William watched as Zack's eyes narrowed, perhaps trying to see if William was being serious. Finally, Zack must have seen something in him and he began to speak.

"The first time if happened was before I was diagnosed. I had been having lots of issues. I would lose feeling in my hands, drop stuff. I was having tremors too, every time I tried to do something that required precision. I couldn't keep my hands steady. I was having a lot of falls, too. There was no explanation for the falls. My doctor recommended physical therapy."

He sighed, and William could see Zack back then, alone and unsure of what was going on. William wished that he had been there for him then. However, William knew that it wasn't the time, that they were meant to meet now.

"I was at work. I was trying to talk to my boss. She was a real bitch, but that's besides the point. It was odd. It felt like my mouth was filled with marbles and fog. My brain knew the words I wanted to say to her…. but I couldn't get them out. I got out one word for every five that I wanted to say. I ended up communicating in hand signals and head nods for a while before she sent me to the hospital."

William shivered. "You must have been so afraid." He pulled Zack in close and kissed his forehead softly.

"I was. I was afraid for a long time. It took them months to diagnose me with multiple sclerosis and get me on the proper treatment. It didn't help that my relationship at the time was crumbling."

"What did your boyfriend say?"

"I had one for a bit when the MS first hit. Then he called me broken and he left. He said he couldn't deal with being with half of a man."

William hugged him tighter. "I hope you know that's not true. You're a complete man to me."

"I know. I also know that he was full of shit. Fear makes people say and do bizarre things." He swallowed thickly. "I'll totally understand."

"Understand what?"

"I'll understand if you want to call things off. I'm a lot of work and unpredictable what with the Multiple Sclerosis. So I will totally understand if you want to end it here."

"You stop that kind of talk right now," William said severely.

"I only meant-"

"I know what you meant. I love you and I'm not going anywhere. I told you I want to know all of you and this is part of it. I love you, Zack."

Zack looked shocked. There was a sparkle in his eyes, and they looked even more like green jewels. "I love you too, Will," he whispered.

"Good." William took a breath. "Glad that's settled. Let's finish looking fabulous. We got a wedding to go to."

Chapter Fifty

Poppy and Dava hadn't talked a lot since going to the Velvet Whip.

There were so many words that they wanted to say to each other. Poppy could feel them burbling underneath her skin when she looked at Dava of when she held Dava in her arms at night.

Poppy wanted to ask if she needed, wanted, desired to go. Poppy could tell that Dava was as uncomfortable with the words they weren't saying to each other as well. The words filled up the room that they were in until it was so full that Poppy felt as if she couldn't breathe.

They were getting ready to meet everyone at the LGBTQ Library. Cordellia had told them all to keep it to themselves, but Poppy had asked her: "What about Nancy?"

Cordellia had chuckled. "Well, of course the dear boy must come and Michael too. You're family after all."

"But he's on his book tour!" Poppy had said.

"Oh dear!" Cordellia had said. "That wasn't well planned of me, was it? Call him and tell him if you can, okay? It would be a shame for him to miss it. He's like a son to me as you're like a daughter."

"I'll see what I can do."

So, Poppy had called Nancy. He had called her back a few minutes later. "What's up, Pops?"

"What's up is that you need to get back home. It's Cordellia."

"Oh my goodness, has something happened?"

"No no, nothing like that. She's all right. It's just that she's marrying Joe this evening at 7PM. She wanted to have you here with everyone."

"Honey, I'm in Montreal!" Nancy said.

"I know," she had said. "She had forgotten that you were away."

"Why is she marrying him so quickly? I thought they were getting married in April of next year?"

"Yeah, me too, but maybe it's a romantic thing, to get married now?"

"I suppose so." He let out a sigh. "I'll see what I can do. But carry on without me if I don't show, okay?"

"Okay, Nance."

"Such a shame too as I wanted to be the flower girl!"

Poppy let out a giggle and she had hung up. That had been hours ago and there was no further word from him. Even Dava was beginning to look concerned; though she always looked concerned lately.

After Poppy checked her phone for the third time, Dava asked "Still no word?"

"No, and we'll have to get to the library soon."

"I know." Dava came closer and pulled Poppy into an embrace.

They stood there with the unsaid words swimming around them. Poppy felt like they were in the middle of a whirlwind. She had to say something or she would likely burst. She had never been very good at holding words inside her when they so badly wanted to break free.

"Dava, listen…"

"No, you listen. I have something to say and I'm not as good with words as you are. When I want to say something, I have to take time to really think about what I want to say."

"All right." Poppy looked at her, wearing a simple dress made out of a deep purple velvet. As Dava paced the room, the dress seemed to sparkle as if it were made of stars. Dava had never looked more beautiful to her right then.

Dava turned to face her and there were no tears, no fear in her eyes, for the first time in a long time. Dava was actually smiling. That sight alone was worth everything that they had been through. The fact that Dava could still smile and that the smile was for her.

"I know that I've been so weird lately, that I haven't been myself. I know you will say that it wasn't my fault and I can't thank you enough for that, but I brought that into our lives through my actions."

Poppy held up her hand. "We'll have to agree to disagree. You didn't do anything to me. Fred did, it's all on him."

"When I think of what he cost us, what he cost you, I almost want to turn to the dark and never return."

"So, why don't you?"

"And miss seeing you every morning when I wake? Seeing you when I go to bed at night before sleep takes me? I live for those moments, for my life with you. I just don't want to be afraid anymore. I don't want to be afraid of what we have and I don't want to be afraid of you."

Taking a deep breath, Dava walked closer to Poppy. When she spoke, it was with a quiet determination. "I don't want to be afraid. I think this might help me. I don't know if S and M is the answer, but it's something I would have control over. Maybe it will help me to truly live again. Are you okay with doing it? With dabbling into something like that?"

Poppy thought of what she wanted to say. When she spoke, her voice was strong, even though part of her was shaking on the inside. "I have to admit some curiosity. And what we saw at The Velvet Whip the other night was…enlightening." She smiled warmly. "But it's something that neither of us has ever done. I would be thrilled to be able to experience it with you."

"I love you so much, you know," Dava said.

"I know. And I love you," Poppy replied.

"Good. That's settled. Now go on and get ready. I'm the only one dressed. We could take you naked; I wouldn't have a problem with that, but that's just me."

"I'd be more worried about where I would carry my money," Poppy said.

They both looked at each other and started laughing in loud, hiccupping guffaws. It felt wonderful to laugh again. Poppy felt a warmth inside of her that hadn't been there since she had carried her baby. It was good to feel that way again

Poppy pulled Dava close. "There's the dirty girl I know and love."

"And don't you forget it." She slapped Poppy's behind. "Oh, I could certainly get used to doing that."

"Yeah, but I'm going to put on some clothes. I think that Cordellia would frown upon you turning her wedding into an S and M orgy," Poppy said with a grin.

Chapter Fifty-One

Romilda watched Cordellia as she got everything ready.

She had never seen Cordellia so sure of herself. She moved with a precision that only she could, graceful and elegant yet commanding at the same time. Cordellia looked as if she were dancing across the room to a tune that only she could hear.

Romilda wasn't ashamed to admit that she still wanted her. Cordellia would always be a person she loved, not only as the mother of their son, but as the woman that she held most beautiful. She couldn't help but be nostalgic for the past, even if Romilda hadn't been her true self then; at least Cordellia had been the other half of her heart.

Romilda's gaze moved to take in the form of Gaston, arranging chairs and tables, making sure the cloths covered everything correctly, that everything looked wonderful. Romilda couldn't deny that she loved Gaston with her whole heart, more than she had loved Cordellia. She shook her head and wiped at her eyes. She was being silly. Romilda should be celebrating the fact that Cordellia's life was finally complete, not lamenting that Cordellia was moving that much further away from her.

It was at that moment that Romilda let go of the love that she felt for Cordellia. Not that she would ever stop loving her, but the romantic love that she fantasised about, the idea or hope that Cordellia would find a way to love her, even though Romilda was no longer the same as she had been. The hope that Cordellia would look at her and still find her beautiful.

Romilda turned and looked out at the stars that were starting to blink in the sky. She sent out the love she had felt for Cordellia in the older part of her life, and let the stars take it. She hoped that when someone made a wish for love, that her love would somehow fall down upon them, making them feel less alone.

Hearing a deep sigh beside her, Romilda turned to find Cordella, wearing a big smile on her face. "How's it going?" she asked, noting how Cordellia looked more beautiful than she had ever looked.

"It's going wonderfully. Gaston is a dream and Justin is a delight. They are both helping me get everything set up. Blaine is helping Joe get ready downstairs. The guys are going to go downstairs and have a mini-stag party. I think that just means they're going to try and get Joe drunk." She smiled. "Thank you for your help, too, Romy."

Romilda had set up some of the chairs and tables for the reception that was taking place in one of the downstairs meeting rooms that were used for book club or AA meetings. She had chosen one where you could see the stars most clearly. "It was nothing."

"It means everything to me that you're allowing me to get married here."

"I did mean to ask about that," Romilda said. "What's the rush? You were supposed to get married next April. I know you want to go on your honeymoon and everything, but surely you've played the rumpleforeskin by now." She gave Cordellia a wicked grin.

Cordellia's face fell slightly, but only for a moment. In that moment, Romilda saw the upmost pain and anguish, the pain that Cordellia was carrying. Then it was gone and a smile was in its place. "Yes, we've had our fun. But we both wanted to do this."

Romilda sighed. "Cordy, don't lie to me. What's wrong?"

"Nothing, nothing at all."

"Cordy, don't bullshit a bullshitter. What is the matter?"

A single tear slid down Cordellia's cheek. She didn't say anything for a moment and in that moment of silence, Romilda loved Cordellia with all of her heart again, no matter what she had sent out into the stars and the heavens. Then Cordellia spoke and said words that shook Romilda to her core.

"He has cancer, Romy." Cordellia took a breath. "He has stage four prostate cancer and there's nothing more the doctors can do. They can't do anything at this point but watch him wither away and die." Cordellia let out a small sob then, holding it back and causing the look of pain to return to her face as she swallowed her pain and didn't let it go free.

There was a sound at the door to the library and Romilda turned to see Poppy and Dava come into the library followed by William and a handsome fellow with green eyes and red hair. She put a hand on Cordellia's shoulder and went to approach them.

"Hello ladies and gentlemen. William, who is this handsome man?"

"This is my boyfriend Zack."

"Pleased to meet you Zack, I'm Romilda Robinson and this is my establishment." She held out her hands as if welcoming him to a night club. "I'm pleased to have you here."

"Thank you for having me. I…have….always to…visit."

Romilda watched Zack's skin blush. There was something there, a further explanation to come, but Romilda knew that now was not the time for it. "Well, you're in luck, Zack. There is no cover charge for tonight. Ladies, I need your help. We have to get Cordellia looking as beautiful as we can. It won't be a lot of work for us as she is already gorgeous. Are you game to come down with me and have a glass or two of wine while we make her look even more beautiful?"

"Of course," Poppy said. "We'd be happy to."

"Excellent. It will be like our own hen do. Now, boys, you will find Gaston over there. Could you help him finish arranging things? The caterers from Talia's will be arriving with food and warming trays to set everything up in about an hour."

"Oh, no, I couldn't let them do that," Cordellia said.

Romilda gave her 'the look' that she had perfected over a long time of asking patrons for late library fees. "You most certainly will. Now come on everyone! Time's a wasting and I desperately need a drink."

Chapter Fifty-Two

Dillon sat across from Josephine Daniels.

She looked different than what he had expected. From the sound of her voice on the telephone, he had thought she would be short and round. He had pictured her with a riot of curly brown hair and several cats nearby, mewing for attention.

The woman sitting in front of him was a svelte blond with a chic updo. She had a fancy necklace on made out of wrought iron and silver and ear rings to match. Jo had dressed herself in a handsome black and white suit coat with matching skirt.

In short, Dillon felt really underdressed.

Dillon held out his hand to her. "I'm so pleased to meet you. Did you already order?"

"No, I was waiting for you. I did order a glass of wine, though."

"Thank goodness. I'll have one too."

"I must say that Rebecca's taste in men has greatly improved. You're quite the looker. Heads and tails above the other nasty man and even better looking than your brother."

Dillon raised an eyebrow. "Why's that?"

"Devon spent too much time brooding, he was always a morose kid, always complaining about something, never happy. You don't look like you would complain about something unless it bit you in the ass. Am I right?"

"Yes, Ma'am."

"I'll have no more of that. Call me Jo. And for the love of all that is holy, stop looking at me like that."

"Like what?"

"Like I'm a shock to your system. Just because I'm close to seventy doesn't mean I have to look like it, does it?"

Dillon shook his head. "No, Ma'am." He coughed. "I mean Jo."

"There you go, you're a fast learner."

The waitress came to take their orders. She left a carafe of wine on the table. "We didn't order this," Dillon said.

"I know. Miss Jo is one of our regular customers. Just a little something for your date, Jo. It's not often we see you in here with a man."

"Well, stranger things have been known to happen," Jo said with that soft bell like laugh again.

When the waitress left, Jo said, "They're very nice here." She held up her glass. "To new friendships."

Dillon held up his glass. "To new friendships." They clinked glasses and took a sip of the wine. Dillon found it to be light and wonderful. He didn't know too much about wine; that was more Devon's territory, but he knew he liked this.

"I suppose you want to hear all about Rebecca and arsehat Jackson."

"And here I thought I would have to pull it all out of you."

"There isn't too much to tell, really. I've been dying to tell someone, anyone. The family won't speak about it and won't speak to her. There's no one I can talk to. It might as well be to you, the man who loves her, so you know what kind of demons she has."

Dillon said, "Everyone has demons. She's told me hers. About what happened with Jackson." He paused, feeling funny to speak a phantoms name. "And about the baby she called Samantha."

"Then if she's told you about them, why do you need to talk to me?"

"Surely there's more to it than that?" He asked hopefully. "Isn't there?"

The food came and they were quiet while the waitress refilled their wine and made sure they had everything they needed. When the waitress left, Jo replied.

"Rebecca is an only child," Jo said. "Did she tell you that? Her parents tried and tried and tried to have more kids. They had plenty of miscarriages but no other children. Rebecca was it."

"Why is that an issue?" Dillon asked gently.

"Well, when she got together with that Jackson asshole, pardon my French, everyone knew that he was bad business. He was bad for our Rebecca and bad for the family. He was a mean man, but he had filled her heart and her head with hope. They were both studying so hard to better their lives. There were so many things that Rebecca wanted to do with her life. We didn't like it when she got pregnant, but you support your family and you take care of your own. But then she told Jackson…"

Jo looked sadly at her plate of pasta and garlic bread. Dillon had never seen anyone look so sad. "He told her that they were too young to have a child and that she would be throwing away her life if she had a baby, and he wouldn't throw away his for her."

She took a slow bite of her food. Dillon's own personal sized pizza sat uneaten. "What happened?" he asked softly.

"Well, you know about the abortion. Her parents were so horrified that she would do that, that she would throw away her chance at being a parent, when they had been trying for so long to have another child. They could never forgive her, nor would they let any of the other family. It was a dark few years, that's to be sure. Poor uncle Alfie came under fire too."

"Why's that?"

"He gave her money, of course. You didn't know that she's worth millions, did you?"

"She's priceless to me."

"And they say that chivalry is dead. No, she was always Alfie's favourite. When he passed, he left her everything that he had. His name is poison in our house, too."

"There must be something I can do. It's been so long, I'm sure."

"It has been almost ten years since they cut her out and not a day goes by that her ghost isn't somewhere in that house. I doubt there's much you can do."

"Please, Jo. I have to try. I wouldn't love her if I didn't try. She deserves to have her family around her, not just her chosen family."

Jo took a long look at him. Dillon felt as if he were being examined and x-rayed. He knew that she was looking at every fibre of him, every hair, every shade of brown and gold in his eyes.

Finally, she took a card out of her purse. There was a name, address and a phone number written there. He looked at the name: Anna Daniels.

"Rebecca's mother volunteers at the local food bank during the week. You can find her there."

"Thank you, Jo."

"Oh, don't thank me for anything yet. I'm a pushover compared to Anna. She will be a hard nut to crack." She reached for his hand and patted it softly. "But if anyone can do it, I think it'll be you. I'm just thankful that you love her so much."

"I'm just thankful that she loves me," he said.

They tucked into their meal. The silence that ensued wasn't one of discomfort. It was one of friendship when no words are necessary.

Chapter Fifty-Three

Blaine took out a bottle of whiskey and put it on the table. "Grooms first!" he said.

Justin and Blaine had set up the basement boardroom to look like a cigar lounge, all dark wood and red velvet. Really just a few pieces of wooden furniture and some lamp shades that cast really low but warm light, but they were working on a tight schedule.

Victoria had heard what they were doing and had added to it, helping them decorate properly, so that the boardroom looked almost like an old lounge club. She had even brought an old record player and some old jazz records. She had brought in a humidor and several bottles of twenty-four-year-old whiskey and scotch.

"Jesus, mom. What are you trying to do? Get them so drunk they can't move on their wedding night? That kind of defeats the purpose, you know," Justin said.

"I don't expect you to drink all of it with Joe, for goodness sake. It's part of their wedding present. As is the humidor, and a ton of Cuban cigars."

"I'm pretty sure that Joe and Cordellia don't smoke," Justin pointed out.

"Ah, but they know people who do, don't they dear?" She shook her hands at him. "Let me do this for them. They've been so kind to me. I want to show them some love in return."

"All right, mom."

"Now I don't want you getting dirty down here right before the wedding."

Justin looked at her in shocked disgust. "Mom!"

"Well, I don't know what you people do when one of your kind is getting married, but in the straight world, they normally hire a stripper. Those are women that take off their clothes," she added, clarifying.

"I know what a stripper is, thanks Mom."

She waved her hands again. "Well, how should I know? I don't know what gay people do for fun."

"Yes, mom, we sit around watching strippers dance for our amusement."

She kissed his cheek. "That's enough of that cheek now, mister. I am still your mother, you know."

"That's pretty hard to forget."

She tapped his hand lightly. "Well, let me know if you need anything. I'm off for a bit before the nuptials."

"What are you going to go do?"

"Sweetheart, just because Joe and Cordellia can't go get drunk before their wedding doesn't mean I can't." She patted his cheek. "Text me if you need me."

"Where are you going to go?"

"Does it matter?" She smiled and wiggled her fingers at him.

Now Justin was wishing that Victoria was still here. Joe wasn't in much of a partying mood and the jazz records seemed to be depressing him. He surprised both Blaine and him by lighting up a cigar. "You only live once," he said.

Blaine watched him smoke the cigar. Joe seemed so down, even though he was about to marry his mom. Something was wrong, Blaine could feel it. It was almost as if with every puff of cigar smoke that Joe blew out into the air, the fog around them increased and became more palatable.

"Joe?" Blaine said softly. "What's wrong?"

Joe looked up and it was as if he were seeing Blaine and Justin for the first time. He gave his head a shake. "Nothing to worry yourself about. Come on boys, have a cigar. I don't want to smoke alone!"

"But you're not having a baby," Justin said lightly.

"But I am marrying the loveliest person on this planet." He handed a cigar to Blaine and one to Justin. "Did you know that I knew your mother a long time ago, Blaine? I've loved Cordellia for over thirty years."

Blaine smile. "Yeah, Mom told me. It's kind of lovely that she found you again, isn't it?"

"More than lovely. It's my own kind of miracle." He saw the whiskey and opened the bottle, pouring out a dollop in three shot glasses. "Come on boys! This is my last night of freedom! Help me pay tribute to a wonderful woman."

Love and Lemonade

They all raised their glasses. "To freedom?" Justin suggested.

Joe shook his head. "Nah, freedom is overrated. Trust me on that boys, one of you better put a ring on the others finger soon. You've found each other, so celebrate that." Joe looked almost wistful and twenty years younger all of a sudden. "Like your mother found me, Blaine."

Blaine held out his shot glass. "To being found," he said.

They clinked glasses and the sound was like bells.

Chapter Fifty-Four

The last person Poppy expected to see walked through the door.

Connie Collins, AKA River Moon Falls, waltzed into the library and looked around. "Gosh, the place hasn't changed a bit. Could use a coat of paint, though."

"So could your face," Romilda said, smiling sweetly.

Connie blinked as if she'd been slapped. "Well, hello to you, your Royal Majesty."

"Hello Connie dear," Romilda said. "Do you still have that stick wedged up your ass? Or has it moved to your hoo hoo?"

"That's for me to know and you to find out," Connie said with a devilish grin.

"Children, children!" Cordellia said. She stepped between Romilda and Connie and put a hand gently on either of their shoulders. "Let's all play nice, okay? This is supposed to be a happy occasion. Besides, Romilda, what would I do if you killed our officiant?"

"What?!" Romilda said. "She's marrying you?" Romilda puffed out her cheeks and huffed out a breath. "Over my dead body."

"That can be arranged," Connie said. "You don't have that much longer left to live anyways."

Poppy came to stand in between Romilda and Connie. "Why do you have to be such a bitch? This is their day. You need to remember that before I bitch slap you into next week."

Connie had the good grace to look somewhat ashamed. "Sorry, Poppy."

"Don't apologize to me. Apologize to Romilda and Cordellia."

Connie turned to look at Romilda and Corellia. "Sorry, ladies. I really am. I just get my back up when I'm in situations like this."

"Perfectly understandable," Cordellia said. "Isn't it Romilda?"

"Yes," Romilda said through clenched teeth. "Perfectly."

"Come on, let's get you a drink. I had Talia's mix us up a special one for the wedding."

"What's in it?"

"Pink lemonade and Malibu rum. It seemed appropriate. I like to call it the panty dropper!"

Romilda let out a choked noise. "Is that really appropriate on your wedding day?"

"Yes, it is. And trust me, Gaston will thank me later! Now come on!"

Poppy watched them walk away and was filled with such a sense of love for the both of them. She turned back to look at Connie. "The officiant? Really?"

Connie gave Poppy a smile. "Yes, really. When you left, I had to do something drastic. I lost the only person that meant anything to me, so I had to find some more meaning in my life…"

"Connie…"

"Hey, it's okay. I was a total bitch. I hated working in the law firm, hated being this ball busting bitch. I was so angry all the time. It's no wonder I drove you into the arms of a man. You just wanted to feel some kind of human companionship."

"Connie, I'm sorry. I really am."

Connie put a hand on Poppy's arm. "Don't be. I'm not. I only hope that Dava treats you like you deserve to be treated. The way that I couldn't treat you because I was so focused on me and didn't realize you were pulling away."

"She does. She does treat me that way."

"That's good then."

"But officiant?" Poppy grinned.

"Hey, River Moon Falls has always been a spiritual being. So it's time for me to own that and to help others find the happiness that I'm still searching for."

Poppy gave her a hug. "I'm proud of you, you know."

"I know. I'm proud of myself." She let out a laugh. "I fucking rock!"

Poppy laughed along with her. "Is there anything I can do to help you set up?"

Love and Lemonade

"Nah. We're a small group, so it should be okay. We'll just make sure that we're good to go and then we can begin. Is everyone here?" Connie said. "Where's the ever-sparkling Nancy?"

Poppy looked around for Nancy and Michael. She had called hours ago. Poppy hoped that they would be able to make it, that they would be here on time. She didn't think that would happen.

"He's on his book tour. I spoke to him. He's in Montreal. I hope that he can make it."

"Honey, don't worry about it. If I've learned anything, it's that stuff has a way of working itself out, you know?" She hugged Poppy close again. "I mean, who would have thought that we'd be talking again? That has to say something, right?"

Poppy nodded and hoped that Connie was right.

Chapter Fifty-Five

"Shit, shit, shit!" Nancy said.

"I don't think there's any reason for that kind of language, now," Lydia said. "Didn't I raise you better than that?"

"Humph. You swore all the time when I was growing up."

"Yes, but do as I say, don't do as I do," she said.

"Yeah, we both know how well that worked out."

"Are you both going to argue all the way back home?" Michael said.

Nancy sighed. He was lucky that his publisher had agreed to change the tour. First Ottawa and then Toronto. It had caused some upset, but when he had gotten Poppy's message, he knew that there would be no way he would miss Cordellia's wedding.

He also knew that there was something wrong. Nancy knew that that could be the only reason that Cordellia and Joe had moved up the date. He just had a feeling about the whole thing. Why move the wedding to now when it wasn't supposed to be until April? He wracked his brain. It wasn't as if Cordellia was pregnant. Why would they move the wedding?

Thankfully, Alyssa had been more than understanding. "Of course you have to go. Surprise weddings aren't anything you would have known about. Besides, they will need a flower boy or two, won't they?"

"Thank you, so much. Beyond words really. The woman getting married was like a mom to me."

"Of course, no thanks needed. Family, even chosen family, is important. You have to honour that."

"Thank you all the same, beyond words."

"Goodness, if you don't have the words and you're a writer, you must be thankful," she had said "Don't worry about it. We can put a spin on it in the media, it'll make you sound even more adorable."

"That's not necessary…do you think it will help?"

"We have to tell them something. People in Toronto have bought tickets." He could almost hear her smile through the phone. "Don't you worry about it. You go and be at that wedding and give the bride and groom my regards. I'll be in touch about the Ottawa event, okay?"

"Okay, Alyssa, thanks so much."

Nancy had been relieved. He knew this was his only chance to see his adoptive mom get married and find her happiness. Nancy would be there no matter what. The relief he felt was short lived however when his mother said that she would be coming along.

"I don't see what the big issue is," she said. "I was going to go with you to Toronto, now I get to see your home and were you live. I've never been to your home, Nancy."

"I know you haven't," Nancy said. He didn't see fit to say anything else.

The car ride had started off quietly but then Lydia had started right up. "I mean, far be it from me when my son moves away from me in a huff and doesn't call, doesn't email, doesn't tell his own mother his address or new phone number."

"Humph," Nancy said.

"I'm just saying! A boy should always stay true to his mother."

"And a man should always stay true to himself."

Lydia let out a short laugh. "I suppose you put him up to this?" she said to Michael.

"Nancy is his own man," Michael said. "It's one of the things I love most about him."

"Funny name for a man, Nancy," Lydia said. "Always thought that was a woman's name."

"It's my name, it's the one you gave me."

"It wasn't meant to be a name, just a nickname," Lydia responded.

"It's the name you mocked me with. I made it my own."

"Oh, that's good. You didn't make the name I gave you your own. Clarence, a fine, strong name."

"You also gave me the name of Nancy, Mom," Nancy said, squeezing the steering wheel tightly. "It's the one I feel more comfortable with. The one that's most me."

"You feel comfortable with a girls name. Silly me, I thought you were a man."

Nancy sighed. "I'm not going to dignify that with a response. What is it you want from me, mom?"

"I want to get to know you. I also want to know why you made me sit in the back seat instead of the front so that I could talk to you."

"You're talking to me now."

"I'm talking to the back of your head."

Nancy pulled over and stopped the car gently. Then he turned to face his mother. "You listen to me. If you continue like this, the back of my head will be all you will ever see of me again. I will walk away, do you understand me? I want to love you, but you're making it so god damned hard. So, you are welcome to come back with us and attend the wedding of the woman who was my mother when you were out of the picture, but you mind me. I will not tolerate any of your crap or your shenanigans, do you hear me? Are we clear?"

Lydia blinked in surprise. "Yes," she said. "I guess we are."

"Good."

Nancy began to drive on when Lydia spoke from the back seat.

"Michael honey, Nancy is so wound up. How long has it been since you've had sex? He clearly needs a release!"

Nancy almost hit the car in front of him.

Chapter Fifty-Six

Cordellia looked around at all the people she loved.

Her son, Blaine, was here with Justin, the man who loved him. There were Poppy and Dava, still both hurting, but drawn even closer for what they had been through. She heard the door open and Chuck walked in with Sebastian and their daughter Cassandra. It was funny to think of Chuck having a child, even if the child was of legal age. Cordellia supposed that people did weird things for love.

It was odd, but she thought of all of these people as her children, in some way. She had looked after Blaine, Mike, William, Poppy and Nancy for as long as she could remember, giving them a home when they needed it or they no longer had one. She had watched them all grow into such fine adults. Blaine and Justin, Poppy and Dava and even Mike and Nancy. Cordellia sighed. She wished that Nancy and Mike were here. She blinked and watched Romilda and Gaston in the corner, making sure that the buffet was all set.

She stood there, all done up for the big event, and realized how very full her life was; and how grateful she was for this moment, right now.

The door opened again and William walked in with his new beau. William had told her all about Zack and she had told him to absolutely bring him along. They were followed by Justin's mother Victoria. She had a man on her arm.

Cordellia walked over to them with a smile. "Victoria, dear. Who is your gentleman caller?"

"Hello Cordy dear. Don't you look lovely! I don't care what they say, there is no reason you can't wear white." She gave Cordellia a kiss on each cheek. "This is Alexander. We met on Hot and Vintage Singles. I hope you don't mind if I brought him with me as my plus one."

"I don't mind. But you better go and tell Justin you brought a vintage stud muffin. He's likely to spit out his drink!"

"Oh youngins." Victoria laughed. "So easily shocked!"

"Don't you love it?" Cordellia laughed and felt lighter than she had all night. She realized that, in a way, she loved Victoria, too. Wasn't she trying to find herself in a world that had become new once again?

"Very nice of you to have me here, Ma'am," Alexander said

Cordellia gave Alexander a stern look. "Now, I don't see anyone here that looks like my mother, do you?"

Alexander blushed, his red cheeks making his silver hair shine all the brighter. "No, Ma'am. I mean, Cordellia."

"That's better. Now why don't you go and meet Victoria's son and get a drink for the two of you?" Cordellia said.

"I'll do that. Do you want your usual, Vicky?"

"Yep, vodka on the rocks, hold the ice," she said with a smile.

"I'll be right back." He gave her a winning smile.

Both ladies watched him walk away. "Victoria, I hope you plan on keeping that man, otherwise, I may have to take advantage of him."

Victoria slapped at Cordellia's arm playfully. "Isn't he a dream? He's dumb as a post, but darling, the potential!" She walked off in search of Alexander and, of course, the vodka. William stood there with Zack.

She saw how proud William was of Zack, how he had his arm around Zack's waist, not in possession but in reassurance. Zack looked really nervous. He kept shuffling his feet and looking up at William, wringing his hands and then looking back at William.

She could see the love that was between them and it did her heart glad that William had finally found his way; that he had found the part of himself that was missing. Cordellia approached him and held out her hands and took his in both of hers.

"My dear boy. William has been all aflutter about you. He talks of nothing but you. You've worked quite a spell on him."

"I-I…I'm s-s-sorry, sorry, th-that wasn't my in…tension." He looked shocked and his brilliant green eyes shone even brighter in fear. He looked like a deer in the headlights.

Taking him in, she wondered what the story was that lay beneath his skin. She knew that she would find out in time if he cared to tell her.

"Dear boy, no, this is a good spell you've woven around our William. You've made him a changed man. Every time I talk to him, he has nothing to talk about except your kindness and the love you share." She gave his hands a gentle squeeze.

Zack blushed and gave her a watery smile. "I'm, I'm, I'm sorry Cordellia. I just…get so…nervous."

"Nothing to be nervous about. You're here on the happiest day of my life and you're welcome here. Feel free to walk around so you can go meet everyone else. William has been keeping you all to himself. Go get yourself a glass of wine and say hello."

"Okay." He turned and gave William a quick kiss before heading off to the bar. William watched Zack walk away from him. William could tell that Zack was having trouble walking because he was shuffling his feet.

Cordellia watched Zack walk away, too. "Will he be all right?" she asked softly.

"I think so. He's so nervous. Meeting my family and everything."

"Well, you just go take care of your man and I'll go take care of mine. It's almost time."

William hugged her softly. "I'm so happy I'm here."

"So am I," Cordellia said. "I wouldn't want to get married without the other man that's been in my life." She gave him a brilliant smile and clutched his arm to her.

"Don't worry, tell Joe I'll share. Plus, your bed is big enough for the three of us anyways." William gave her a wicked grin as she pulled her hand away and smacked him hard on the arm.

Chapter Fifty-Seven

Curtis wondered if the world had changed or simply looked different with a ring on his finger. He kept looking at it, thinking it would somehow disappear, and then looked over at Devon, thinking he was a figment of his imagination.

Both the ring and Devon remained. He hadn't imagined it. It had really happened. Curtis snuggled closer to Devon and looked at the ring again.

"Gosh, if you're like this now, wait until I put a wedding ring on your finger," Devon said.

Sucking in a breath, Curtis let it out and looked at Devon with shock. "What do you mean?"

"What do you think I mean?" Devon took hold of the remote and pressed a button. Devon took Curtis' hand that wore the ring and stroked it softly. The movie they were watching was paused and Devon thought it was at a good place. Wesley and Buttercup on screen and Wesley had just said, "As you wish."

"I gave you a promise ring, not a wedding ring, not yet. I asked Rebecca what kind of romantic gesture I could make, and she suggested a promise ring. She also suggested that I could give you my pin, but I had no idea what that meant. A ring seemed a good idea, a symbol of the love that I have for you and the bond we have together."

Curtis could only nod. He wanted to speak, indeed he had so many words that he wanted to say but could find no voice in which to give them. He could only look into Devon's dark eyes and hope that he could see the love that filled him so completely.

"I screwed up once, I let go of a love that I cherished beyond what I thought possible. Now you've come along and shown me how to love beyond even that. I didn't think a love like we have was possible."

Curtis found words pouring from his mouth, as if they had only been waiting for the right moment, not lost within him. "Me too. Every other man has tried to change me, make me lose weight, make me stop doing drag. I'm so glad you haven't tried to do that to me. That you love me, even despite my eccentricities."

"I love all of you," Devon said. "I don't really understand the drag thing, but that's part of you and I love it."

Curtis shrugged. "It's my way of engaging with life, you know? Kind of like your hooking, except with no sex. It's my way of expressing myself, of being creative. I'm not an artist or a writer, or a musician. I am also not a woman trapped in a man's body. I know that. I like my penis. I love my trans friends, but I know that isn't the life for me. It's more about imitation being the sincerest form of flattery."

Love and Lemonade

"You're so good at what you do. That's one of the reasons I love you. You're so authentically you in everything that you do." Devon took Curtis' hand that wore the ring and kissed it. "It's not a wedding ring. Not yet. But I hope you can wait until it is. I promise that it won't be too long."

"I've waited my entire life for you. I don't mind waiting for you to be ready. Besides, we just met each other. Don't you want to get to know me first?"

Devon smiled. "I know everything I need to know right now. We have years to get to know each other, Curtis."

Curtis leaned forward and kissed Devon. "You're perfect for me."

Devon laughed. "Oh, I'm far from perfect." "Don't misunderstand me. No one is perfect. I said that you're perfect for me."

Chucking, Devon said, "Well, all right then!" and kissed Curtis back with everything he had.

Chapter Fifty-Eight

Looking at Rebecca's mother was almost eerie.

She had Rebecca's oval face and jaw and cheek bones. She had her dark eyes and straight black hair. Rebecca wore the look better, though. She had more life in her eyes. Anna may have looked like Rebecca, but she had none of Rebecca's beauty, her vivaciousness. None of the spark was there within her.

Anna looked tired and they hadn't even talked yet. He wondered if she existed in a state of fatigue. He wondered if being so angry made a person old before their time. He could see that there had been beauty there once, that at one point in her life, Anna had been beautiful.

Now, Anna just looked washed out and so very tired. He hoped that it wasn't just Rebecca who had made her look so angry, but he had a feeling that it was.

She pursed her lips before she spoke. "So, Jo told me that you wanted to speak to me about Rebecca." She took a sip of white wine and said no more than that.

"I wanted to start by saying that I love your daughter."

Anna raised her eyebrows. "I would assume so; otherwise, you would not be here."

Love and Lemonade

He took a sip of his own glass of red wine. She had wanted to meet at a restaurant called Wilfred's. The waiter had come to take their orders. He had ordered a Caesar salad with grilled chicken. He had hope that was a safe choice. Anna had ordered the lobster and the crab salad with truffle oil dressing. Devon had ordered one glass of red wine and she had ordered a bottle of white for herself.

He knew that Rebecca's family had money and he was trying not to judge her mother, but really, ordering a whole lobster for herself and the crab salad while sitting there dripping with diamonds and other precious gems, was a little much. The fact that the jewelry she was wearing shone so brightly made Anna look even more pale in comparison.

Dillon told himself to remain calm, that yelling at her wouldn't do any good. "I know what happened. Jo must have told you that. I know what happened with Jackson and with Rebecca. She told me about the abortion. Did you know that she has never stopped regretting that choice? That she is still beating herself up for making that choice, instead of showing the baby the love she had been denied?"

"Yes, we told her that Jackson was a no-good reprobate."

"I'm talking about you."

The first sign of a crack in her face appeared. Anna raised her eyebrows even further. "Me?" She sounded scandalized. "But we're her parents. We did nothing but love her."

"No, you didn't," Dillon said. He took a sip of his wine and made her wait for a further reply. When he spoke again, it was difficult to get the words out without sounding angry. "You didn't love her the way a mother should, unconditionally. The moment she made a choice you disagreed with, you cut her out, sent her away."

"I hardly think-"

"No, you don't think, do you? She still misses you. I can hear it in her voice. I can see it in her movements. You know she wants to adopt a puppy? So that she has someone to give her love to."

"What about you?"

"I get plenty of love. But she has so much love to give and not many people to give it to. She needs her parents."

The waiter brought their food. Dillon later liked to imagine the face that the waiter had made as he put all of the food in front of Anna. He nodded at Dillon as he left. Dillon sucked back the rest of his wine in one shot and stood up.

"It's been *lovely* meeting you." He didn't bother keeping the sarcasm out of his voice.

"Aren't you forgetting something?" Anna said.

Dillon turned back. "What's that?"

She gestured at the meal. "A gentleman always pays for the meal."

Dillon let out a snort. "Yeah, and a mother usually loves her daughter unconditionally," he said and walked out of the restaurant, leaving Anna wearing a shocked and disgusted look on her face.

Chapter Fifty-Nine

The rest of the car ride wasn't as stressful as it had been.

Nancy relaxed and was more himself with his mother. Michael knew that the two of them had a lot to work out and work through, but he was happy to let them do it and gave them space; well, as much space as he could give in a car and with Lydia in the back seat.

Lydia's last comment had brought out the much-needed laughter that was inside of Nancy. Michael hoped that he was remembering the joy that his mother had brought him. Though any relationship is difficult, none is so difficult as mother and son.

A mother wants to love you unconditionally, but she also has to be the protector, the teacher, the wise woman. A mother has to be the warrior, the sage, the counsellor. She also has to be the drill sergeant and the authority figure. If she's lucky enough, a mother becomes a friend.

Michael didn't know where Nancy and Lydia were on their journey, but he hoped they were closer to finding that out for themselves. He was happy to drive while Nancy and his mother talked. Nancy was turned around in the front seat so that he could talk to her.

"Do you remember that time I came home to find you messing around in my closet? You had on one of my wigs and had put on some of my makeup."

"I did that more than once. You just didn't know it," Nancy said.

"Nah, I knew every time after that first time. I could feel your touch on my dresses and wigs. It was warmer somehow, you know? I liked knowing that when I wore those pieces after you, it was like taking a bit of you with me."

"Why would you get so mad at me when you found me dressed up or when I used your makeup?"

"Are you kidding me? Even at that young age, you were able to put on eye liner better than I could and my colours looked better on you than they did me!" Lydia let out a loud belly laugh. "Oh, honey, you came out of my closet wearing one of my beehive wigs and a scarf draped around you like a toga that had hippos on it. I nearly busted a gut laughing, you looked so wonderful."

"I think all gay boys wear their mother's clothes at some point," Michael said.

"True, honey, but not every child could do it with such *style*!" She let out another laugh. "You should have seen my Nancy. He came walking out of the closet one day, wearing my clip-on earrings and a white scarf that I used from time to time, only he was wearing it as a skirt. He did the best Marylin Munroe impression that I've ever seen. I nearly wet myself when he did that!"

Love and Lemonade

A genuine smile was on Nancy's face. "I remember that!"

"You came out singing diamonds are a girl's best friend, but you did it with a bit of a drawl, that somehow made it all that much better. You were my little mimic back then Nancy."

"I would have liked to see you walking out of the closet," Michael said with a grin.

Nancy slapped his arm softly. "Shush you, no comments from the peanut gallery."

"Oh Nancy, this one has sass. You better hold on to this one."

"I know mama. I plan on it."

They drove up to the GLBT Library and all three of them got out of the car. Lydia looked at it and smiled. "It's filled to the brim with books, I suppose?"

"Libraries usually are, Mom."

"Don't be a smart ass, Nancy honey. It doesn't suit you."

"But he does have a smart looking ass," Michael said laughing.

They both slapped him, each on a different arm. "Behave yourself, or I'll hose you down. Don't think I can't do it!" Lydia said, smiling.

Michael and Nancy laughed and they joined hands. Michael felt stronger just holding on to him and he hoped that Nancy felt the same way.

"I can't wait to see everyone. It feels like we've been away for so long, but it's really only been a few days," Nancy said, giving Michael's hand a squeeze.

"I know!" Michael replied, giving Nancy's hand a squeeze back. "I can't wait to see Cordellia and Joe! I can't believe they're getting married, that they've waited so long to find their happiness."

"I hope Dava and Poppy are okay," Nancy said. "I know they've been going through a lot since the loss of the baby."

"I know. I hope they're okay too," Michael said. "Do you think Blaine has killed Victoria yet? Or did Justin intervene?" Nancy let out a laugh and they walked a little further on, the doorway to the LGBT Library in sight.

Michael heard Lydia's footsteps stop behind them and he stopped to turn and look at her. Nancy stopped with him.

"Lydia? What's the matter?" Michael asked.

"Oh, shit," she said. She threw her hands up in the air. "I've really screwed things up, haven't I?"

"Mama, what do you mean?" Nancy said softly.

"I've just made a mess of things, that's all."

"What are you talking about Mama?"

"Nancy, don't you see? Hearing you talk about these people, well honey, they're your family. Even I know that."

"Of course they are, Mama. They are the family I chose when I had no one else," Nancy told her.

"But honey, *I'm* your family. I'm your mother."

"I know Mama. Chosen family or not, you will never stop being my mom."

Michael watched the two of them look at each other. There were still a lot of words left to be said, but they were getting there. They were doing a dance of emotions. The dance towards forgiveness was one of the longest. Nancy and Lydia had a long way to go, but they had started. That's what mattered.

Nancy hugged his mother close. Michael saw tears in her eyes that made her eyes look as if they were made of glass.

"Come on, Mom," Nancy said. "Let's go meet everyone."

Chapter Sixty

Cordellia stood under the awning that Blaine and Justin had put together with Romilda's help. It had been covered in ivy and in the candlelight, if she squinted her eyes, it looked as if she were in a forest. Cordellia wondered if it was appropriate to feel like a fairy princess at her age and decided that age didn't matter. Princesses were forever.

Romilda and the boys had strung fairy lights on the shelves and along the ceiling. Cordellia didn't think that she had ever seen anything more beautiful than this moment. But then she saw Joe standing at the end of the isle and changed her mind.

She had never seen anything more beautiful than Joe, right at this moment.

It didn't matter that he was sick, that their time was now limited, that everything was uncertain and unknown. All that mattered was Joe and the love that they had between them that had lasted for beyond thirty years.

The moment was broken when the door opened to the right and behind Joe. Nancy walked in to the library followed by Michael and a beautiful woman. Cordellia wondered who she was and made to approach them when Nancy waved at her. "Later," he mouthed and then he gave her a huge, bright smile.

Now the room felt complete. Her heart was bursting with love for everyone in it: Justin and Blaine, Romilda and Gaston, Chuck and Sebastian and their daughter Cassie, Victoria and her beau Jackson, Dava and Poppy, William and Zack and even Connie, though she could often be a stone-cold bitch; Cordellia supposed that was part of her charm. She looked at each of them and took them all in.

Then she turned to Joe and felt that love increase a hundred-fold. She held out her hands to him and he came to her willingly.

His hand clasped hers and she felt his warmth. She imagined that she could feel his heartbeat in his hands, that the love he felt for her was filling her up to the brim. Cordellia felt a tear slide down her cheek.

"Are you okay?" Joe asked.

She nodded. "Better than okay. Right now, at this moment, I'm happier than I have ever been. I love you so much."

"And I love you," Joe said.

They turned to Connie. She smiled at them and Cordellia was surprised by the warmth that she felt from her. Maybe she was working on her happiness after all?

"All right, bitches! Let's get this show on the road!"

Then again, thought Cordellia, maybe not. She saw Poppy slam her forehead with a palm and let out a big sigh.

Connie gave her a bright smile. "Just joking. Do you mind if I just wing it? I mean, I could read from the script if you want me to, but I think I know you well enough to speak from the heart. Would you let me do that?"

Cordellia looked at Joe. "What do you think?"

He thought about it for a moment. "Hey, this is the only time I'm getting married, so we might as well make it interesting."

They looked at Connie and nodded. "Go for it. Try and keep it PG, though, won't you?"

"I'll do what I can," Connie said, giving them both a small grin.

For her part, Cordellia was wondering if giving Connie free reign of the ceremony was either the smartest or the stupidest thing she had ever done. Well, it was too late now, she thought.

"We're gathered here today to celebrate the love of two people," Connie said. "I've known Cordellia for a long time. In all that time, she has been a mother to most of us in this room, a friend, a confidant. She has been a pillar of strength, a guiding force in our lives and a balm to our souls."

Connie took a breath and Cordellia reflected that she was really touched by Connie's words.

"She finally listened to her heart and let it lead her towards happiness with Joe. He is the other half of her heart, the piece that had been missing for so long."

Love and Lemonade

Cordellia stole a glance at Romilda and expected to find her looking upset, but instead Romilda was smiling at her, tears in her eyes that were left unshed, making Romilda's eyes glassy in the half light. She was comforted by that sight.

"Cordellia loved Joe a long time ago," Connie continued. "Madly in love, she still chose to leave him and be a mother to her son, Blaine. She chose to be alone and raise her child, thinking of him rather than herself. Yet, today, she is finally putting her heart first. The heart doesn't know about years or days or age. The heart only knows about love and I can tell that Cordellia's heart is full to the brim with love right now. Doesn't she practically shine with love, folks?"

Cordellia was moved by this. She hadn't known that Connie had known about her past with Joe, that he had filled her heart even then. Looking at him, she saw that he was practically shining with the love that he felt for her.

"For his part," Connie said, "Joe waited a long time for Cordellia. Almost thirty years. So strong was his love for her, his knowledge that he had already met his soul mate, that he chose to wait for her rather than find someone else. For she had already taken part of his heart; Cordellia only had to return for his heart to be complete again.

"And now, here we are today, to unite these two hearts as one, to strengthen the bond between them. To celebrate love."

There was a hush in the air, so full of words not said but felt. Filled with wanting and worship, lust, life and love.

Cordellia was moved by it, she held on to Joe and knew that he felt the same way. She could feel his heartbeat through his fingers, as he could feel hers, and she wondered when they had become the same beat, the same tattoo of rhythm?

Connie reached out with one hand to grasp Cordellia and Joe's clasped hands and gave them a squeeze. She looked at them. "Do you have the rings?"

Cordellia nodded and Blaine brought them forth. He handed one to Cordellia and one to Joe. They each slid a ring on each others ring finger. When that was done, Connie smiled.

"The couple have chosen not to say vows, stating that everything has already been said between them. Instead, they want to get right to the cake and then the fucking. Whatever floats their boat, folks, am I right?" Connie said.

Cordellia saw Poppy smack her face again. Cordellia laughed a little. Connie had been doing so well.

Letting out a snort and a laugh, Connie gave Cordellia and Joe a wide smile. "I'm just kidding you. I couldn't be happier. I know that holds true for everyone else in this room. You may kiss your bride Joe."

When Joe leaned in to kiss her, Cordellia felt like her heart would float her away, like she was in a dream. She stood there with his ring on her finger, his heart in her hands, her heart in his; she was surrounded by everyone that she loved and stood with the man that she loved most of all. It was everything that she had ever wanted and she had never been happier.

She kissed Joe again and he wrapped his arms around her as if to keep her as close to him as possible. She let him pull her close and thought: *I guess, like a true princess, sometimes good things do happen.*

Chapter Sixty-One

Zack had enjoyed the ceremony very much.

Seeing two people so much in love, that their love was the only light in the room and the real lights paled in comparison; how wonderful that would be to experience. He hoped that someday, something as wonderful would happen to him. He wondered if it would be with William?

He was so afraid. So very afraid. William was smart and talented, kind and wonderful. Zack wondered why a guy like William would saddle himself with a man like him. But then, hadn't William said that he loved him? Didn't love conquer all, at least according to the storybooks?

The men he had known were not nice men. They tried to fix him, tell him what he could do to better himself with his MS. They never stopped to even ask Zack what he wanted, or what he was doing to better his life. Hadn't he changed his diet three times, cutting out all sorts of foods that were known to cause inflammation in the body? Didn't he work out three times a week, doing an exercise routine that had been designed for him by a rehabilitation fitness expert? He was swimming now, at least twice a week, and he had taken up meditation and positive thinking, knowing that stress and depression were some of the worst things for MS.

That hadn't mattered for those men. Zack had still been broken, had still been considered a burden. He had resolved to spend the rest of his life alone, sure that no man in his right mind would want a man like him.

And then along came William.

He hadn't read any gay fairy tales, but he supposed he could write his own, or talk to Nancy. He thought about it. No, he supposed it was better to tell his own story, to lay it out on the page if he was ever called to do so, not call on anyone else to do it for him. Zack was living his own story, so he would tell his own story.

Looking for William, he saw him sharing a word with Connie and Cordellia. He smiled to himself and went to get a drink of punch. Looking at it, the punch seemed to have been made from pink lemonade and about a gallon of vodka.

He was still having trouble walking. He had been stressed and nervous all evening and hadn't thought to ask William to get him a chair in case he needed to sit down. Zack was really wishing for his cane. His steps were wide and unsure, and he was off balance a little bit. He could feel eyes upon him, real or imagined, as he went towards the punch bowl. Zack's overstressed body gave a lurch and he fell a little into a woman who steadied him before he could fall.

"Woah there son, are you okay?" The woman asked.

"I'm...just going....to...get some...punch," he said, almost forcing the words out of his mouth.

"Son, I think you've had enough. Did you have a few before you came to the wedding? Don't blame you, but still."

"I'm not…drunk."

"It's all right if you are. Few people know when to stop these days. Here, let me sit you down."

"I'm…NOT…DRUNK!" He was almost yelling now, almost spitting with each word. It came out louder than Zack had intended. Now other people were looking at him. He could feel their eyes on him like hot needles, each one burning his skin.

"Honey, it's all right if you are. But I think you've had enough, I really do. Did you come with anyone?"

Zack let out a scream of rage and frustration. His legs felt like they were going to give away at any moment and he was becoming lightheaded. He felt spasms starting in his legs from standing for so long and was looking around for a seat when he felt hands take hold of him.

"It's okay, Babe, it's okay. I've got you. It's okay."

It was William, gorgeous and lovely William of the thousand books. Beautiful kind William. He relaxed a little in his embrace. "I need…chair."

"Okay Babe, it's okay. Nancy, could you?"

There was the scrape of chairs and then he was sitting, the chair was gloriously comfortable because he was sitting and William wasn't shying away from him, wasn't running away. "So…embarrassed. Sorry, I'm…sorry," he said.

Love and Lemonade

"No, don't you dare," William said, gently taking Zack's face in his hands and kissing him softly. "Don't you dare be sorry, okay?"

He stood and looked at the woman that Zack had knocked into. "Who the fuck are you?"

The woman held herself up straighter. "I am Lydia and I am Clarence's mother."

William let out a scoff. "You mean Nancy? His *real* mom just got married," he spat. "I don't know who you think you are…"

"The gentleman fell into me. I'm afraid he's had enough to drink. It's okay, there's no harm done," she said, looking flustered.

"But you see there is harm done. You've harmed him. Zack is my boyfriend and he has multiple sclerosis. He's not fucking drunk."

William put his hand on Zack's shoulder. "Babe, did you want a drink?"

Zack nodded, a tear sliding down his face. "Yes please. I'd…like some…of the…punch."

"It's my recipe," Cordellia said. She had come up to stand in front of Zack. "It's made with pink lemonade and a *lot* of vodka. It'll be good for whatever ails you."

"Okay," Zack said.

William leaned down to kiss Zack on the lips and Zack felt warmth spread through him. Not just from the kiss, but the fact that William would kiss him in front of all of his friends and family. "I'll be right back, Babe."

Zack nodded and looked up at the room. It was silent and every eye was upon him. "S-sorry. So s-sorry."

"Don't be sorry, my dear boy," Cordellia said. "Will you come and dance with me? It would make me so glad."

"Can't...dance."

"I'm sure that's not true." She extended her hand. "Come on dear, let's show these people how its done."

Zack smiled and took Cordellia's hand. He was surprised. She could really lift his weight. He blushed when he stood completely. "S-sorry."

"Oh, you shush. There's nothing to be sorry about, dear boy. You just hang on to me and we'll cut up the rug."

"Won't J-Joe mind?" Zack asked. "He's sup-posed to get f-first...dance."

"We have the rest of our lives to dance together. He won't mind if we have just the one dance."

Zack nodded and walked towards the dance floor, his hand in hers. When she faced him, he was struck by how sad she looked. The look was gone in an instant before anyone else could see it.

"Don't be sad. Please," Zack said.

Cordellia looked at him and smiled, her lashes wet. "My dear boy, with such a handsome man for a dance partner, how could I be sad?"

Chapter Sixy-Two

Mike watched Zack and Cordellia dance.

He also watched William. They stood beside each other with Nancy nearby. Nancy was talking to his mother about something and they hugged briefly.

It should have been weird being in the same room as William, but it wasn't. It felt different. He was different. William looked as if he was a different person. He appeared older somehow, more centered. More balanced than Mike had ever seen him before.

As Mike looked at William, he felt none of the old feelings or the anger that he had been filled with when he thought of William. Instead, Mike was surprised to find that he was only filled with happiness.

"So," Mike said.

William turned to look at him. He only saw Joy there. Mike's eyes had lost the dead look they had had for so long when William was being hurt by David. His eyes had lost the hardness that they had had when William and Mike were together.

"So," William said.

They watched Zack and Cordellia dance together. There was a moment where Zack looked as if he would fall, but Zack righted himself and looked over at William. The love that shone out of Zack's eyes brought a lump to Mike's throat.

"I'm really happy for you," Mike said softly.

William smiled. "I am too. More than you could ever know." He shrugged. "Actually, you probably do know. I'm sorry that I couldn't love you this way when we were together."

Mike shook his head. "Don't worry about it. Things happen."

"If you say for a reason, I'm going to smack you," William said, grinning.

"No, not that. Just…things happen. You and I weren't meant to be together the way you are with Zack."

"We only just met." William blushed.

"Meh, whatever. I know love when I see it."

"Well, you do have love with Nancy," William said. "I never thought that would happen, but you're both so happy together." William motioned to the ring that Mike wore on his left hand. "Did you get engaged? Did he propose?"

Mike shook his head. "Nah, we just wear each other's rings for now. That's what Nancy wanted."

"What do you want?"

"Well, I have him. I have my family, my friends. They really are my chosen family, you know."

"I know. But you didn't answer my question."

"No, I didn't." Mike's face broke out into a wide grin. "Well, Nancy doesn't know it, but I do plan on proposing.

Just not right now. There's so much going on and we're at Cordellia and Joe's wedding. I don't want to steal their thunder. "

"I'm happy for you, William."

"And I'm happy for you."

They didn't talk very much after that; they had reached the part of their relationship where words weren't necessary. They just looked at the people dancing. Joe had gone on the dance floor with Cordellia and Zack was walking towards them. Mike smiled when Zack was in front of them.

"I'm sorry, Will. Cordellia can really dance!"

"Don't be sorry and stop apologizing. I was just talking to Michael. We go way back."

"I know." Zack smiled and said, "I hope he didn't talk your ear off."

"Hey!" William said. "You're supposed to back me up."

"I am!" Zack laughed and leaned in to kiss William. "Did you want a drink?"

"I wouldn't say no to some of the pink lemonade punch if there's any left."

"Cordellia said there are a few vats of it so that we can go all night."

"Excellent. Then bring me a tall glass and we can look at the buffet. I'll meet you back here."

"Okay. Nice meeting you, Michael."

"Likewise," he said with a smile. He watched Zack walk away and then said softly "So, multiple sclerosis." It wasn't a question.

"I know," William said. "We all have our challenges that we have to overcome. That's his."

"What do you plan to do?" Mike asked softly.

"Support him any way he needs it." There was a pause that was filled with words. Michael knew what words they were, but thankfully William didn't leave them unsaid. "I plan on loving him as much as he'll let me. I have never met anyone else like him."

"That's good, William. I'm happy for you."

"Thanks. That means a lot." William looked uncomfortable for a moment. "I'm sorry."

"For what?"

"For not giving you what you needed. For not giving you what you wanted, not being able to love you as much as you deserved."

Mike shrugged. "Hey. Shit happens." He gave William a smile. "And look what's happened to you. I'm proud of you, you know."

"Yeah?"

"Yeah. I am."

"Thanks, I'm proud of myself too."

There was a moment where Michael wondered if he should say something else, anything else. Though their relationship would never be the same as it had been, he hoped that tonight they had taken the steps towards salvaging whatever was between them. He thought that they were on the way to becoming friends. Mike guessed he couldn't hope for more than that.

Zack was back and carrying two glass goblets filled with pink lemonade punch. He handed a glass to William and then Zack took William's free hand with his own. They walked into the crowd of dancers and Mike smiled after them.

Nancy came up behind him and put his arms around Michael. "Did you meet William's new beau?" he asked.

"I did."

"Did you like him? Zack?"

"I do. I think he'll be really good for William. They're already so far in love. It really is wonderful to see."

"Awww, muffin! Our little boy is all grown up!" Nancy teased.

"I know! It happened so fast! Their never young for very long."

Nancy leaned in and kissed Michael softly on the lips. The kiss was soft and his eyes were open and searching. "You okay?

"Yeah."

"I'd understand if you weren't. You shared a lot with him.
"

Michael shook his head. "I liked William quite a lot. Maybe even loved him a little. But I've always been in love with you. I couldn't give him my heart because it already belonged to you."

Nancy kissed him again. "Good answer honey. Now how about we go get our own drinks. I want to get sloshed and have you take advantage of me later. I've been a very bad boy!"

"Sounds like you could use a spanking!" Michael teased.

Chapter Sixty-Three

Devon couldn't believe how happy he was.

He tried to think if he'd been this happy with Nancy, and he didn't think so. Much as he had loved Nancy, it hadn't been enough for either of them. He hoped that, wherever Nancy was, he was happy, that he had someone who loved him.

He was up before Curtis, so he figured he would make himself useful and put on a pot of coffee. Devon was just putting the water in the machine when he heard Curtis behind him.

"Well, that's not a sight you see every day!" he said, gleefully. "You seem to have forgotten your clothes."

"What's the matter? Don't you want some buns with your coffee?" he teased. He gave his buttocks a saucy little shake and was rewarded with the sound of Curtis' laughter. Then Devon felt Curtis' hand on his hips pulling him close.

"It's all good. I forgot my clothes, too!"

"Oh, you saucy minx!" Devon turned on the coffee maker and was rewarded with the sound of the coffee brewing. He turned and looked at Curtis, expecting him to look joyous after such an amazing evening, but he looked contemplative instead, looking at the silver ring on his ring finger.

"What's up? You look all serious," Devon asked.

"It's just…I don't know, I love you, you know I do…"

"Ugh, will I like where this is going?"

"It's just, this is great and you're fabulous, but what happens now?" Curtis looked concerned.

"What do you mean?" Devon asked. He was starting to feel like he had lost the thread of the conversation somewhere along the line.

"Just that I got to bed thinking of you…"

"Well that could be because we usually cuddle before bed."

"…and I think of you first thing when I wake up."

"Again, usually because we have a cuddle in the mornings. Where is this going, Curtis? Where is this coming from?"

"Just that you've given me everything I never thought I'd have. It's almost too good to be true, you know? I'm afraid that when I wake up one morning that you'll be gone and I won't ever see you again. Is that silly?"

Devon thought he understood, now. Curtis was afraid. He had only known hurt and ridicule, pain and heartache. This was all new for him, for both of them. They were both entering into unknown territory. Devon thought he could put Curtis' mind at ease. He hoped that it would work.

"I've been thinking," Devon said.

"A dangerous thing to do," Curtis teased.

"I'm a rebel that way. Roll with me here. You can't stop thinking of me and I can't stop thinking of you. Your wearing

my ring now. We've been together for a while now. I think
we take the next logical step."

"We get a dog?" Curtis asked.

"No, turkey. We live together."

He had expected Curtis to break out in joy, but that fearful
look on his face deepened. "Do you think that's a good idea?"

"I think it's a fabulous idea. Don't you want to wake up
every morning in our own place?"

"Yeah, but live together?"

"Babe, we pretty much live together now. I'm always at
your place or you're always at my place." He took Curtis' face
in his hands and kissed him. "I want to build a life with you.
That generally means that we have to live together."

Curtis nodded. It took him a while to find his voice. "But
what if we fuck it up? I mean, neither of us is relationship
material."

"Says who? Why don't we do it and prove all those voices
in your head wrong?"

"But what if we fuck it up?" Curtis asked again more
quietly.

"Honey, we probably will fuck it up at first because we
don't know what we're doing. But isn't that the glorious mess
of life? Don't you want to experience that kind of life with
me? One that's filled with dinners at home, being woken up
for morning sex, falling asleep in our place? Don't you want
that with me?"

One corner of Curtis' mouth curled up. "Well, I do like the sound of morning sex…"

When they kissed, Devon could feel the tension melt out of Curtis' body and when the kiss ended, he pulled Curtis to him, trying to emote through touch. Curtis was warm and he was everything to Devon.

"So," Curtis said, "now that we're moving in together, can I look for a puppy? Oh! Better yet, we could get our own pony!"

Devon kissed him again and kept on kissing him.

Chapter Sixty-Four

Upon entering the GLBT Libarary that morning, Romilda was greeted by the mess of love. More like the mess of a wedding that no one bothered to clean up, but that didn't matter. She wasn't picky. Love was love in whatever form it took.

Romilda loved the early morning. She was the first one in and the last to leave. She loved having the library to herself. It was her baby, after all. After Cordellia had left, she'd had no one. They had stayed together until Romilda had gone to have her surgery. When she came back, Cordellia had taken Blaine with her and she hadn't seen them again for almost a decade.

Those had been lonely years. Romilda didn't know what she would do, hadn't known how she would survive. Then the option to buy the building came up. It had been used as a sex shop for the gay village and had sold such things as dildos, panty hoes, blow up dolls. There had been slings and whips and condoms and lube. It had done a roaring business, but Romilda had always stayed away. She didn't go in for all of that kind of stuff. She wanted the love, the affection. She wanted Cordellia and she was gone from Romilda's life.

One day, that all changed. She had been walking home from her job at a call centre and had seen the for-sale sign on the front window. The slings and whips and sex toys had all been cleaned out or were being sold off for cheap.

Romilda entered the store for the first time and marvelled at this size. The place could have fit any number of small businesses but that's not what she had had in mind. She knew right away what the building was good for, what it was meant to be.

The owner, a guy by the name of Gus, had owned The Boom Closet forever. When Romilda approached him, he looked up with a smile on his face. "Hey Ro. What do you know?"

She had shrugged. "What I'd like to know is why you're finally closing. Had enough of the sex trade?"

"Yeah. You wouldn't believe some of the sickos that came in here, especially after we started having private rooms and porno booths. And the fucking mess! If I ever see another blob of spooge again, it will be too soon. What brings you in here?"

Romilda looked around and imagined the walls of books, maybe even a small café, to help contact the visual image of a pool of spooge. Romilda cleared her throat. "I'm interested in buying the building, actually."

"What, you want to run a sexy joint?" Gus asked with a slight leer. "I never pegged you as the type, Ro."

"Gods no. I have something else in mind entirely. I want to open a GLBT Library."

"It'll never fly, honey."

"That remains to be seen. How much is the building?"

"I have no clue. Bank took it and they're selling it for a song."

"Why did the bank take it?"

"Couldn't make payments, could I?"

Romilda gave Gus a shrewd look. "But this place made scads of money. There were always customers here and you were always ordering stock."

"Yeah, but after a while, most of the profits went up my nose, didn't they?"

"Oh," Romilda said. "I see."

She had gone to the bank the very next day. She had spent the previous day and evening mapping out a plan for the library that she saw in that building, the types of services they would offer, the community that they could reach. She mapped out a complete business plan and a general idea of what the next few years would look like, the funding she could wrangle up with the rest coming from her own pocket.

Romilda also pulled together her finances. Looking at the number on the screen, she hoped it would be enough. It would have to be enough.

She went to the bank. She had booked an appointment with one of the people responsible for the building. Romilda hoped that they would show pity on a defenceless old woman…well, defenceless and old were a stretch, but she was a lady, damnit.

Walking into the bank, she had approached the front desk. "Hello. I have an appointment with Eldecot Johnsen."

Romilda shivered.

It was hard to believe that a simple meeting with a man had changed her life, but it had. She had her home, the books, her son; sons, if she was truthful, as that's what Blaine and Justin were to her. She had Corellia back in her life, in whatever way that was, at least she was back in Romilda's life.

The library had given Romilda that. She would not lose the building to some asshole who thought his dick was bigger than everyone else's. She wiped away a tear when she heard the door open behind her. "You're a little early, Blaine. I hope you brought coffee," she said.

"Well, I don't have coffee but I do have something else you used to enjoy."

Turning, she saw Eldecot Johnsen, standing in the doorway to the library and grinning at her like she was five ounces of fried chicken. "What the fuck are you doing here?" Romilda barked at him.

"I came to look at the place before I demolish it. It's nice to have a moment or two to observe it as it was before it's torn down to the pile of rubble that it will become…unless of course, you've had time to think of my offer?"

She smiled her most evil smile. "Oh I've had time to think it over, in amongst other things. Did you know that my ex-wife got married here yesterday? That she married the man she loves who is going to die soon anyways? That even though she knows he's going to die, she married him? It was a joyous occasion, full of family and togetherness."

He actually had the gall to laugh. "I'm sorry I missed it."

"I'm not. Now, I also did a little digging of my own. It seems you're married now, isn't that correct, mayor Eldecot? To a Beatrice Prud'homme."

"What of her?"

"What would you do if I were to let her in on our conversations? She'd be very interested to hear what you have to say, don't you think?"

He shook his head. "I don't think so, no. She's roaming over the beaches of Tahiti at the moment. All she cares about is her next Mai Tai."

Romilda let out a curse. That had been the ace up the sleeve. She walked towards him. "I still don't understand why. You've risen from a lowly bank manager to the mayor of our little town. I am eternally glad that you've helped me in the past as you have, making sure that my application got approved. Always have friends in high places, that's what I always say. But that was years and years ago. We had fun in the sack and a few other places that come to mind. I just don't understand."

Eldecot came towards her, almost slinking his way along the shelves. "Isn't it obvious?" He held out his hands as if commanding an empire. "I mean, I know you loved grand gestures to get your attention. Isn't this grand enough?"

"You got my fucking attention. Now what the fuck do you want?"

"Isn't it obvious, Romilda? I'm still in love with you."

Before she could respond, the front doors opened, and Gaston stood there, holding coffees and looking confused.

"Romy?" He gestured to the mayor. "You let me know if you need me to throw him out for you."

Chapter Sixty-Five

Dillon woke to the slamming of a door and the banging of pans on the kitchen counter. He hadn't known either of those sounds to herald anything good, so he pulled the covers up to his chin and hoped that whatever mood Rebecca was in would pass.

When he heard the breaking of glass, Dillon knew that he had to get out there. His mother had taught him a lot of things, but chief among them was the knowledge that if he heard the slamming of a door, the banging of pans and the shattering of glass, he had screwed up somehow.

Gathering his courage, he went to see what was wrong. Rebecca was sweeping up the glass and greeted him with a wide smile.

"Oh, hello Dillon! I've made you some coffee! Would you like some!"

She never spoke in such a cheerful voice this early in the day, so Dillon knew that something was wrong. Of course, with all the banging and all the noise, it didn't take a rocket scientist to figure that out, never mind the fact that Rebecca never cooked.

"What are you doing? Can I help you with something?" he asked, cringing inwardly and the fear in his voice.

"Oh no! I don't need any help from you! I've made you a coffee and have made you breakfast! I made you some scrambled eggs and bacon with homemade fries!"

"Thank you," he said softly. He waited…and waited. He didn't have to wait long.

"I made scrambled eggs, each broken shell broken like my fucking heart. And I burned the fucking bacon, because I wanted it to resemble the love that I have for you that is burning me up inside because I'm so fucking angry. The homemade hash browns were just because I needed to chop something with a very big knife, over and over again, picturing your face as I did it!"

"Oh," he said.

"OH! I hope you're hungry darling! And if you tell me you don't want to eat it, you better leave the fucking kitchen! Better yet, leave the fucking apartment! Leave the fucking *world*!"

Stepping carefully, Dillon walked closer to her, trying to look as if he was ready to be comforting. He had a feeling that he knew what this was about. "Rebecca honey, if I leave the world, I'd be dead and I wouldn't be able to eat the fabulous breakfast you've made me."

"Oh, now that would be a fucking shame! Wouldn't it just?! Well fuckadoodledoo!"

He knew that she was furious. She was saying 'oh' a lot, something she did only when she had to calm herself down;

that and she was looking more maniacal as every moment passed. "Honey, what's wrong?"

She came close to him, moving with a speed that Dillon didn't even know she possessed. "How fucking dare you! How *dare* you! You know who I got a call from this morning before I started making you this shit-tastic breakfast? Huh?! Do you?"

"I think I have an idea."

"My fucking mother! My stupid bitch of a mother who called me to tell me that the next time I wanted to talk, not to send my fucking boyfriend."

"She knew that you didn't send me. I told her that you had no idea I'd come."

"What?" Confusion was now spreading over her face, replacing the anger.

"I wanted to find out what had caused the rift between the two of you. I met your aunt Jo and she told me what you went through, what that dickhead did to you. What your mother did after he had hurt you so badly."

"What? You talked to Jo?"

"I did. After that, I talked to your mother. I told her that anyone that would turn their back on their daughter when she needed her the most, wasn't a mom and wasn't mother."

"Why would you do all of this?" She motioned at the air in front of her as if encompassing the whole world. "Why, Dillon?"

"When you told me that your family cut you out, I knew that there was more to it than that. I could also see the hurt you tried to hide, could hear the pain in your voice." Dillon paused. "I wanted to see if I could alleviate that pain."

A tear slid down her cheek. "Maybe I just wanted a fucking puppy."

"Yeah, well…" He ran his hands through his hair. "I'm sorry."

"Why are you sorry?"

"What do you mean?"

"I've never had anyone love me enough to find out so much about me. Not even fucking Devon knew about everything you do. It's like you've opened me up and read what's written inside."

"I love you, Rebecca. I want to know and love all of you, even the dark difficult stuff. That's part of who you are."

"I love you too. However, to make it up to me for doing all of this behind my back, we're going to have Devon and Curtis over and we're going to go get a puppy." She smiled. "Okay?"

Dillon looked at Rebecca, really took in the measure of who she was. Her dark hair was a riot of curls and it framed her face, making her look almost angelic. Her green eyes flashed with an intensity that never failed to get his heart beating faster. He knew that he would do whatever he could do to heal the crack in her heart and that he would love her for as long as she let him.

Love and Lemonade

"Deal," he said. "Now let's go *out* for breakfast, okay?"

Chapter Sixty-Six

Cordellia didn't know when she had been happier.

There was a sadness underneath the joy, a melancholy that resided under the warm glow of the happiness that she felt. Still though, she had never been happier as she was at this moment. She looked at Joe as he cooked breakfast for her and she watched as he moved. It was like he was dancing.

Joe had always been this way. He moved as if he was made of music. He had a fluidity in his limbs that made her feel like a clumsy fool when she walked beside him; but when he took her in his arms, it was like her body responded to the music within his and they could both dance together as they moved.

When she had left him, Cordellia knew that she was leaving behind that music because the music belonged to Joe. In a way, she had been listening for the song his body created all along. Now, their song was a crescendo of notes and beats. She could hear the music within her.

As Cordellia watched Joe, the music in her swelled so that it was all she could hear above the beat of her heart. When he turned to face her, though, the music came to a slow ending. The silence seemed final, somehow.

"Joe?" She went to him and took his hands in hers. "What's wrong?"

Love and Lemonade

"Why would you think anything is wrong? I'm the happiest that I've ever been, right now in this moment."

He kissed her softly on the lips and when he pulled away from her, she could see it in his eyes. There was a finality there and she knew that the music within him did not reach his gaze. She placed a hand on either side of his face and tried to look deeply into his eyes, but he kept avoiding her gaze.

"Honey, what's wrong?"

He shrugged. "Let's enjoy the first day of marriage without any talk of horrible things, okay?"

"No. We're not starting out our marriage that way. You need to tell me what's wrong," Cordellia said. She tried to keep the mom sound out of her voice but knew that she was not entirely successful when Joe looked as if he had been smacked. "Sorry about that. I don't know where that voice comes from."

"Never mind about the voice, it's the look that frightens me."

"Sorry, Joe."

"Don't be sorry. Once a mom, always a mom." He kissed her forehead and pulled her close.

"Tell me what's wrong," Cordellia said. "Please."

He grimaced and pulled away from her a little bit. He took a while to answer her. "You know that I'm ill."

"Yes, Joe. Of course I do."

"Well, I've been talking to my doctor."

"Is there a new treatment?" she asked, ashamed of the hope in her voice.

"No, darling. There isn't. But there are options that I have."

"What options are those?"

"Well, I don't want you to have to watch me waste away. No one should have to see that."

"But I want to." She stopped. "No, that came out wrong. I don't want to, but I'm your wife. We stand by each other through everything. That's what we're supposed to do."

"And what? Have you watch me waste away until I'm a skeleton of the man that I was before, forever changed in your eyes?" He shook his head. "I can't put you through that."

"Joe, it's okay."

"No, it's not because *I* don't want to go through that. I can't go through that. I won't put you through it either."

"Then what are we going to do, Joe?"

"I've already talked about it with the doctor. He said that there's no pain and I won't feel a thing. That I'll be able to pass peacefully, sparing all of us any pain."

A tremor filled her heart and the song within her that was his skipped a beat and then hit a sharp note. "Joe, what are you talking about?"

He kissed her softly then, as if trying to find the words and not finding them, communicating with a physical action. When he pulled away from the kiss, it was the tears in his eyes that frightened her more than the cancer that his body was riddled with.

"I've chosen to take my own life. I think the doctor called it assisted suicide."

Cordellia's heart stopped. "No, Joe, I can take care of you, I will take care of you. Let me do that for you, please."

He shook his head. "It's already been decided. I've talked about it with the doctor. I will not go through the end that way and neither will you." He kissed her forehead. "Neither will you."

They held each other then. All Cordellia could smell was his cologne and all she could hear was the tumbling of flutes inside of her heart.

When he took a deep breath, so did she, not able to find the words that wanted to break free from within her.

The air was filled with the scent of burned food. She would always associate the smell of burnt eggs with the moment her world had fallen apart.

Chapter Sixty-Seven

"I fucking hate you," Cassie spit out.

Chuck didn't know if it was directed at him or at Geoff who was sitting across from her. Sebastian stiffened. "Honey, is that any way to talk to the father of your baby?"

She let out a rough laugh. "Ha! All he did was put his dick in me. He is less of a father than you are, Mom."

"Ouch," Geoff said.

"That was a low blow," Sebastian told her, looking hurt. "Just because you are angry doesn't mean you have to be rude."

She huffed out a breath. "Fine! Whatever."

"You're certainly acting like a legal adult at the moment," Chuck said.

"Whatever, this is your fault," Cassie snapped.

Chuck motioned at her stomach. "It's my fault that you got pregnant?"

"No, but-"

"Well, so do I get to choose the name of the baby since it's mine?"

"No, but-"

Love and Lemonade

"Oh! I know! If it's a girl, I'll name it Consuella Poutine Fiesta! If it's a boy, I'll name it Jim Bob Daniel Dave Brown!" Chuck actually clapped his hands.

Sebastian gave him a look. "Are you done?"

"Almost. I just thought of another name for a girl! Lady Cher Gaga! Wouldn't that be amazing?"

"You know, you're really gay when you gay the fuck out," Cassandra said.

"I know." Chuck gave her a big smile. "It's part of my charm."

Cassie turned to look at Sebastian. "Is there any way to turn him off?"

"Nope," Sebastian said.

"Look, can we talk about the baby?" Geoff said. "That's why I'm here."

Cassie looked at him with a sour look on he face. "You don't get to speak."

"That's not really fair," he said.

"No, you know what's not fair? My boyfriend walking away from me when I told you about my fucking dad. You just walked away. So, you don't get a say and you don't get to speak."

Chuck cringed inwardly. This wasn't going at all well. He had telephoned Geoff's mother and told her about Cassie's pregnancy. He never expected Geoff to show up on their doorstep. Didn't kids nowadays text or email instead of eye to eye contact? Colour him surprised.

Hoping to defuse the situation, Chuck invited him in and had him sit in the living room so that he wasn't visible when Cassie came down stairs. However, as soon as Geoff had heard her footsteps, he had gone right to her. And here they were. Chuck wondered if there was such a thing as a gay standoff?

"Look, I do get a say. It's my kid and I love you. That's all that matters," Geoff said.

"Oh, you love me, do you?" Cassie stood and towered over Geoff who was sitting down. "Then why did you leave? Because of my freak of a mom?"

"Hey!" Sebastian said. "You're being a bitch, you know that?"

"Sorry, I'm just trying to make a point," Cassie said.

"Well, then make it."

Geoff stood and paced back and forth a little. Chuck had done that walk when he had told Sebastian that he had loved him. He knew that Geoff was a bit of a dick, but Chuck could tell that he genuinely loved Cassie.

"Look, I know I was a shit, okay? I know it. My parents asked me what happened between us, and I was a dick, but a baby changes thing, don't you think? It's something that we created together."

"The less said about the whole creation process the better, thank you," Sebastian said blandly.

"The thing is, I was wrong." He looked relieved. "There, I've said it. Can we get back together now?"

Love and Lemonade

Chuck looked at Geoff and rolled his eyes. "Oh honey, it takes a lot more than just saying you're sorry."

Cassandra stood and Geoff, Chuck and Sebastian all stepped away in fear. They knew that staying in the line of fire was a bad idea. Sebastian and Chuck moved away, leaving Geoff to be the sitting duck.

"You come back here and tell me you're sorry and you want to get back together, just like that? By saying you're SORRY?" Her eyes looked as if they were on fire and they made her red hair look as if they were made of flames. She slapped Geoff across the face and then did it again with the other hand.

She let out a breath and smiled. "There, I feel better." She walked into the kitchen to pour herself a decaf coffee.

Geoff looked at Sebastian and Chuck. "Should I go after her?"

"I'd leave it for now. It's enough that she allowed you in the apartment. Just give it time. She'll come around."

"Yeah, and you still have your balls," Chuck said. "I'd say that's a win-win!"

Chapter Sixty-Eight

Nancy reminded himself that murder was illegal and that it would be difficult to get that much blood off of the hardwood floors of their apartment. Oh, and Mike might mind, just a little bit.

He turned around and looked at her. She scoffed, "Don't you look at me that way. I am your mother. All I asked for was some espresso. Normal coffee is too weak for me."

"I'm sorry that what I have on hand is not to your liking. Maybe you can go home and get your own damn coffee."

Letting out a laugh, Lydia said, "Is that all you got? I thought you gays were supposed to be all sassy and shit? Don't you people know how to sass back anymore?"

"Well, speaking as the spokesperson for my people-"

Michael came into the kitchen and stood between the two of them. "I can't leave you two alone for a moment, can I?"

Nancy pointed at his mother. "She started it." He tried not to pout and wasn't entirely successful.

"Aw, Babe," Michael said. He pulled Nancy into an embrace. "You were both doing so well. You had gone one whole evening without a fight. What started this one?" Michael knew that they needed to fight, but he didn't want to watch Nancy do something or say something that he would regret later.

"My mother accusing Zack of being drunk."

"Honey, that was last night," Lydia said. "I apologized after the wedding and told him how sorry I was. He was okay, so was Devon. I must say that your taste in men has improved greatly." She gave Michael a saucy wink.

"Um, thank you?" Michael said, blushing slightly.

"No, thank you. For showing my boy what a real man can do. You do your mother proud," Lydia said.

"Um, okay?" Michael wasn't sure how to respond to that.

Nancy got right up in Lydia's face and snapped his fingers. "As if you would know. You come here and take one look at Devon and you judge him as beneath me? You take one look at the life I've built with Michael and decide that he's perfection?"

"Oh, Nancy boy. Why are you so angry still? After all this time?"

"Yes. After all this time."

"Well that makes two of us. Do you think I wanted a son like you? Don't you think I wanted grandchildren? Don't you think that was what I deserved?"

"What about Shelagh? She could give you babies, couldn't she?"

Lydia let out a strangled sound. "She's like you."

"What, she likes to suck cock?"

"No. She…goodness, I can't even say it. She likes women the way you like men."

Nancy stared at his mother and for a moment, silence filled the room. Then, slowly but quickly gathering steam, Nancy started to laugh. It started as a giggle but then spread into a guffaw and slipped into belly laughter. Soon, Nancy was doubled over, laughing so hard that tears were pouring out of his eyes and he had to hang on to Michael for support.

"It's not funny," Lydia said quietly.

Michael let out a hiccup of laughter at that moment, too.

"It's really not that funny." Lydia said. She was frowning now.

Michael let out a howl of laughter that he had been holding in and Nancy's laughter was renewed in a new flurry of belly laughter. He couldn't see his mother through the tears that were flowing from his eyes.

Lydia put her hands on her hips. "When you are quite finished."

Michael tried to take a few deep breaths and slowly got himself under control. Nancy did the same. Taking a few deep breaths as well, Nancy ran a finger under both of his eyes. "Mom, thank you."

"For what?"

"For the best fucking laugh I've had in a very long time. I haven't laughed so hard since Devon told me he had a ten-inch penis and it turned out to be six inches long."

"You mean I'm bigger?" Michael asked, looking somewhat chagrined.

"You know it Babe," Nancy said.

"I don't need to hear about your ex-boyfriend's penis," Lydia said.

"No, you know what? I don't need anymore of your shit."

"Watch your language!"

"No, you watch yours. You are in my house now. I am done being treated like a second-class citizen because of who I love. The fact that I'm gay is only a small percentage of who I really am. What about Shelagh? What does she think of your worldly views?"

Lydia looked away from them. She looked saddened. When she spoke, her voice was soft and unsure of itself. "She won't talk to me," she said quietly.

Nancy let out a bark of laughter. "Why would that be? Do you talk to her like you've talked to me my whole life? You call me Nancy Boy. What's your name for her?"

Lydia wave a hand. "It doesn't matter."

"What's your name for her?" he asked again.

"Clam Digger," she whispered. A tear slid out of her left eye.

There was silence in the room again and this time there was no laughter to follow it. It hung in the air like a music note un-played, like a story untold.

Nancy calmed down. There was a calmness in his eyes that Michael hadn't seen before. Nancy approached his mother and placed a hand on her shoulder. "I can't get angry at you anymore. I just can't. I know that's what our whole relationship has been about, always fighting, always trying to get the other to be what they wanted. I wanted the mom that baked cookies. Instead, I had you. You smoked all the time and you would go out drinking and singing karaoke in clubs, trying to relive your glory days of when you sang. You wanted a straight kid who's only purpose in life was to fill yours with grandchildren that you could spoil."

Nancy placed his other hand on her other shoulder and looked at her. Really looked at her. "I feel sorry for you," he said. "Me and Shelagh, we've found who we are but you're still searching for the woman you left behind. You're looking for the you that doesn't exist."

He kissed he forehead. "I love you Mama, but I don't know if we're good for each other. I spent ten years of my life wondering what I would say to you and I can say only this: I love you even if you don't love me."

"Oh Nancy, I love you. I've always loved you."

"You had a shit poor way of showing it." He took a deep breath. "Now, enough of this. You need to decide what you want and who you are. Michael and I have to get ready for my friend's exhibition."

"Aren't I coming?" she asked.

Nancy shook his head. "No, Mama. I need time away from you. And I don't want you accusing Zack of anything again.

I think it will take a while for William to forgive you for that. Me too, come to that."

Nancy stepped away from her, each step hurting to do it. It felt like he was leaving a part of himself behind. Michael took his hand and it was as if Nancy had regained a part of himself. "We'll be back later, Mama," he said.

Then they left Lydia alone.

Chapter Sixty-Nine

Blaine reminded himself for the fortieth time not to be nervous. He then told himself for the fortieth time that that was bullshit and to commence the widespread panic.

He could do this, he could do this, he could, he really had no choice, sure he did, he could walk away, leave the room, go out and get shit stinking drunk, ignore the world, ignore everyone.

"Babe, take a breath," Justin said.

"I don't know what you mean," Blaine said.

"Look, I know you're nervous."

"No, I don't want a coffee right now," Blaine said. "Just a scotch and soda would be nice."

Justin put both of his hands on Blaine's shoulders and turned Blaine around to face him. "Take a breath for me."

Blaine did so.

"Now another one."

Blaine took another breath.

"There. Feel better?"

"Much, thank you."

"You can do this, Blaine. You have no idea how talented you are. You're a brilliant painter, a master at it. Everyone will love them."

"But what if they don't? I've only ever painted for myself. No one but you and my family has ever seen them."

"So?"

"So, what if I'm no good? What if all I do is crap?"

"You aren't crap, and you know it. You got this, Babe. You so got this." Justin kissed Blaine softly and felt Blaine melt against him.

Blaine sighed happily. "Thank you."

"No thanks needed. Someone has to talk you off the ledge and it should be me."

"How can you believe in me so completely?"

"Because I've seen your work, heck I've seen you at work. You aren't here on the physical plane when you paint, Blaine. You're someone else, somewhere else, when you paint. And what you can create is incredible."

"You have to say that, you're sleeping with me."

"No," Justin said. "I don't have to say that, but it helps."

Blaine put his arms around Justin and pulled him close. "How is it you know exactly the right thing to say?"

"Just a talent I guess."

They kissed again, and Blaine felt a little bit of the worry fade from him. He took some of the strength that Justin gave him. Justin always seemed so strong to him, so sure of himself. Blaine knew without a doubt that Justin had his back, no matter what happened.

"What would I do without you?"

"I don't know, go crazy and wear plaid and striped pants?" Justin said jokingly.

Blaine smacked him lightly. "Even if I was crazy, I'd be far more fashionable than that!"

"Oh, so you'd wear a plaid shirt with a flower printed skirt?"

Blaine smacked him harder and kissed him again. The kiss was cut short when they heard the sound of footsteps on the hardwood.

"Making out again? I do envy the high sex drive of you gay people. It puts me to shame! Jackson may be younger, but he's a once a night kind of man, not this two or three times a night kind of guy like you gays are!" She let out a laugh that sounded like a hyena that had sniffed helium.

"Hello Mother," Justin said, going to her and kissing her on the forehead. "I'm just happy to see you happy."

"Isn't it lovely? I'm getting more action in the sack now then when I was married to your father. He was a once every *month* kind of guy. Didn't have Jackson's stamina." She gave them a wry grin and a wink.

Justin let out a laugh and Blaine looked as if he were going to be sick. "I'm happy for you, Mom."

"Yes, but if I could only convince him to go down on me. I've always loved it when a man loves a bit of muff diving."

Blaine let out a howling noise. When Justin looked over at him, Blaine was doubled over in laughter, clutching his sides. Victoria looked at Justin.

"Was it something I said?" She looked at them with a wide grin on her face. "Get your minds out of the gutter, boys. We've got a lot of work to do before the week is up. Do you realise your exhibition is in a few hours?"

Blaine went slightly green. "Don't remind me. I'm so nervous. Before I had the wedding to focus on, but now the exhibition is just staring me in the face and I don't know what to do."

Victoria went to him and took his hands in hers. "Blaine, darling, you don't have to do anything. You're the artist. You just have to talk to people, give a little speech and then stand back and watch your paintings fly off the wall. Simple as that dear boy."

"Crap, I have to talk to people *and* give a speech?" He looked even more green. "I really don't think I can do this."

"Just think you're looking at your next subject for your next painting," Victoria said.

"What, picture them naked?"

"Goodness no, that would give you nightmares. Just pretend you're painting them as you talk to them, that should relax you."

"That might not be a good idea," Justin said.

"Why's that?"

"Blaine tends to lose focus on reality, and all that exists is the painting in front of him. Plus, he tends to drool as he paints."

Blaine slapped Justin's arm. "I do not."

"You do too. Why do you think I keep wiping your chin?"

"I thought you were trying to be sexy."

"Well, yeah, that too, but you do drool."

"Hmmm," Victoria said. "Drooling on potential customers could put them off of your art. That could be problematic." She thought about it for a moment. "Well, maybe you better picture them naked after all. At the very least, it will be like watching porn, and we all know you gays love your porn don't you?"

She grabbed a scarf, purse and sunglasses, not noticing or caring about their shocked looks. "Jackson is picking me up and we're going to go have Mai Tai's. Later boys!" she said.

Chapter Seventy

Dava took a deep breath for the first time in a long time.

For a while now, she felt as if she couldn't breathe, couldn't get air in. She hadn't been able to see past her own face, hadn't been able to focus on anything except her own fear. What she was afraid of, she didn't know. Fred was in prison for battery now and would be for some time to come.

She had been afraid for a long time, even when she was away from Fred, there was always the chance that he would come after her, or after her boys. She wasn't worried for herself, but only those that she loved.

Then the unthinkable happened, the moment she had been preparing for, and all because she had dared to wake the beast. All because she had taken the step that she should have taken years ago. She knew that there was a possibility that he would come after her when she had him served with papers, had known it in her heart.

Dava didn't regret any of that, but was still heartbroken over the fact that Poppy had lost her baby. Dava still hadn't forgiven herself. The fact that she was responsible for the ending of a life that had been growing inside of Poppy and was now gone, well, that was something that she would have to carry with her. Dava would have to forgive herself.

However, she felt freer than she had felt in a long time and that was thanks to the support of Poppy and her friends. Mostly it was due to her taking back control of herself, even in small ways.

The S and M helped greatly. They had been back to *The Velvet Whip* a few times now, even during the daylight. While Dava wasn't sure that she would be able to bring it into her home yet, she was tempted to try. She had bought a whip and a couple of masks. She wanted to start small and save the big stuff for the club for now.

The truth was, she felt free. There was something empowering about either giving up control or having someone give it up to you. It was about trusting someone so completely and being able to have them trust you in the same way.

That was what she had with Poppy. She knew what she had to do. It was so clear to her now and she knew that this clarity was because of Poppy and the life they were going to build together.

When Poppy came into the room, Dava went to her and wrapped her arms around Poppy. She inhaled her scent, something spicy and the scent of oranges. Dava kissed her softly and said, "Thank you."

"Well, you're welcome, only I don't know what I'm being thanked for."

"For not giving up on me. For not letting me retreat into the shadows when all I wanted to do was hide."

"You're welcome, sweets. Its what girlfriends do."

"Except, that's the thing. I don't want to be girlfriends anymore," Dava said.

Poppy paled and her skin nearly shone, framed by hair that was red like fire. Dava wanted to kiss her so much at that moment, knew that she would do anything for her. She finally truly understood.

"What?" Poppy's voice was a whisper.

"The thing is, I want more. I want everything that I've been too afraid to get, too afraid to claim it for myself. I thought I was worth nothing, now I know that I deserve everything."

"Well, that's…" She didn't finish. Dava wouldn't let her.

"The thing is, my everything is you. You are my everything, my past, present and future. You are everything that is beautiful and I want to grow older with you. You've shown me what it is to truly live and you came into the dark to find me and bring me home. I want to build my home with you."

A tear slid down Poppy's face. "What is it you're saying?"

"Will you be my wife? Will you marry me? You are the other half of me that I didn't know that I was searching for. Be mine, please."

Poppy looked at Dava and smiled brightly. Leaning forward, Poppy kissed Dava softly on the lips. "Of course."

Then Poppy reached behind her and pulled out the whip that Dava had bought. "But first, you have to be punished. I thought you were breaking up with me!"

"I guess I'm not good at marriage proposals either," Dava said smiling, thinking Poppy's disastrous attempt. Dava felt a lick of heat pass through her at the thought of Poppy running that whip over her skin.

Skin she finally felt at home in.

Chapter Seventy-One

Romilda turned and looked at Gaston.

She took all of him in: his silver hair that brushed his shoulders, his blue eyes that were right now shining like steel. Her whole body thrummed for him and she knew without a doubt what was about to happen. She would make it happen. Romilda was through being intimidated. She had been that way her entire life, told that she wasn't woman enough, that she wasn't worth enough. Now here she was with two men fighting over her and only one man was going to win; the one that held her heart.

"Romy, I mean it," Gaston said. "You let me know if you want me to throw him out."

"How much have you heard, dearest?" Romilda asked him.

"All of it."

"Excellent. Mr. Mayor, I don't accept your offer," she said.

"I'm sorry? I'm afraid I didn't hear you correctly." Eldecot narrowed his eyes, glaring at her.

"Oh, so now you have selective hearing, do you? Let me repeat myself. The answer is no." She crossed her arms and thrust out her chin.

"Your forgetting something. I'm the mayor, I can have your building shut down permanently. This library will cease to exist."

"Actually, Mr. Mayor, you're wrong. I own this building. Everything is up to code. You'll find that I have my up to date business licence and building specs in my office. You'll find that everything is in order."

He scoffed at her. "So? I have the right to shut down any building I want to. But you can save this building. All you have to do is come back to me."

"Why would I want someone with such a small penis? I need a Cheerio , a magnifying glass and a pair of tweezers to find that thing you call a dick." Romilda smiled sweetly at Eldecot. "No offense."

"You fucking bitch!"

Gaston moved to throttle him. "Don't you dare talk to her that way!"

"Don't touch him, Gaston. He's not worth it."

"Now your showing some sense!" Eldecot sneered.

"No, I'm stopping you from getting your ass kicked. You also can't knock down this building. The entire community would be up in arms. Everyone comes here. It's one of the oldest libraries in the city and it's the only GLBT one left. If you knocked it down, it would hurt your chances for re-election."

"I'm not worried about that. Those idiots are like sheep and they do what they're told. So, you will if you know what's good for you."

Romilda stepped right up to him and she was so close, she could almost kiss him. "I feel badly for you. Imagine having to threaten a woman just to be with you. It's sad, really. It also says a lot about you. That you need a woman to be afraid, that you want a woman to be begging you not to destroy something that she's worked so hard for. You would reduce her to nothing. Do you get some kind of sick pleasure out of that?"

"You always did love the sick stuff," Eldecot said with a leer.

"Not anymore I don't. But you know what hasn't changed?"

"What's that?"

"My ability to be prepared." She reached into the pockets of her dress and pulled out a small tape recorder, its tape running.

"What is that?" Eldecot hissed.

"Oh, so you're stupid as well as having a small dick? This is a tape recorder and its been recording everything we've said."

"You're bullshitting me."

"No, I'm not. I saw you coming on the surveillance cameras. I pressed record and popped this in my dress, thinking it may come in handy. You do anything, anything at all, to my library, and I will make sure that the right people find this tape."

"You fucking bitch!" He said again. He grabbed her arm that was holding the recorder.

Gaston came up behind him and grabbed his arm, pulled it back. "You better leave now, sir. You can't handle a woman like that. That's not right."

Eldecot pushed away from both of them, glaring with wild eyes. "If one word of that tape gets out, so help me!"

"Yeah, yeah. Now get lost. It's almost time to open," Romilda said.

Eldecot went, spouting swear words the whole way. Romilda was surprised that the paint didn't peel off the walls from the language that he was yelling. When the doors closed, she let out a sigh of relief.

"Thank goodness," she said.

Gaston wrapped his arms around her. "I'm proud of you honey. You showed that man who's boss."

"I sure did. He ought to know by now not to mess with a lady."

Romilda let out a laugh and turned to Gaston, kissing him softly.

Chapter Seventy-Two

Michael wondered how he could love two such stubborn people.

He loved Nancy with all his heart and soul. Always had, even when he had been with William. There had always been a flame that burned bright for him that Michael had tried hard to keep snuffed out. Despite his best efforts, that flame would pop up again and again, dancing in the wind of his desires.

Despite how odd it might be, Michael had to admit that he loved Lydia, too. Despite her horrible behaviour, she had raised an amazing man. Nancy wouldn't admit it, but he got most of his sass and verve from his mom. Watching the two of them together was proof of that.

"Why did you come back?" Lydia asked. "Felt bad for leaving me all alone and defenceless?"

Nancy's hands curved into fists. "You are far from defenseless," he spat out.

"Now, come on you two. I dragged Nancy back here so that we could put things right. But let's start off with something simpler. Lydia, did you have a question for your son? Maybe about his book tour?"

"Oh, yes." She turned stiffly and tried to put on a smile. "What's happening with the tour? Did you talk to your publicist?"

"I did. I was supposed to do Toronto and then Ottawa, but now I'm doing the reverse." Each word was like a bullet. "I have an author appearance next weekend."

"I'm so happy for you, Nancy. Truly. I always knew you'd do great things."

Nancy looked moved, despite his resolve to remain impassive. "Thanks, Mom."

"I should probably write a memoir myself, now that you're famous. I could tell the story behind the bitch."

Nancy stood and was about to scream some obscenity, but Michael stopped him. "Lydia, that's enough. Why do you have to goad him on like that?" Michael dragged a hand through his hair. "I lost my mother years ago. I would give anything to be able to talk to her again, to tell her what is going on in my life. I would give anything to have the chance that you and Nancy have." He looked at both of them, trying to make his meaning clear. "Don't throw away the chance that you've been given. You have each other in your lives again. Celebrate that."

Nancy looked somewhat ashamed and Lydia looked mollified. They didn't look even close to celebrating but they weren't yelling at each other. That had to be a step in the right direction.

Love and Lemonade

Lydia took a deep breath and then another. She closed her eyes, as if she was facing some internal battle that only she could hear. When she spoke, it was without the sass or the attitude. Michael thought it was the first time he had heard her real voice.

"Nancy, honey, do you know why I'm so hard on you?"

Nancy's eyes widened in shock. He shook his head. "No, Mama. I don't. I've never known. Sure, we had our good times, but we always fought, all the time."

"Your grandmother said it was because you were the most like me. You were always a lover of life, very carefree, wanting to explore. Your grandmother and I had the same problem. We fought all the time. She often wished that I would be blessed with a child that was like me and she got her wish, more than tenfold."

"So that's why? That's why you don't like me, because I'm like you?"

"Oh Baby, of course I like you! I love you unconditionally, but I even like you most of the time and the two are not remotely the same thing. You can love someone, but that doesn't mean you like them very much. I both love *and* like you, Nancy."

"Then why, Mama? Why were you always so hard on me? Why did you push me away but pull me close?"

Lydia took another deep breath, but she did not close her eyes this time. She looked at her son and he looked back at her. "I suppose it's because you're gay."

"Mama-"

"Now, let me finish. It's not the fact that you're gay, lord knows I knew you were gay at five years old, the first time you came out of my closet wearing one of my wigs and a set of my clip-on earrings. You had even dabbed on some lipstick, too."

"That doesn't make me gay, Mama."

"Oh honey, I just *knew*. You know? It wasn't the fact that you were gay. It was the fact that people would hurt you because of who you loved."

There was a ringing silence in the air after those words. Nancy reached across the table and took his mother's hands in his. "What do you mean, Mama?"

"Honey, I know you go around all sparkly, but the world is a cruel place. When you came out of the closet, I knew that you couldn't be hurt in something random, like a car accident, a plane crash or some random injury. Now, you could be hurt, even killed, because of who you are and who you love. That frightened me more than anything you could possibly imagine. I knew that I had to toughen you up some, put some sass and verve in amongst all that beautiful sparkle. If I came across as a little harsh, it was a small price to pay."

Nany sat there looking at his mother, really taking in her face, the lines upon it that told a story that only she could fully tell. "A little harsh? Really Mama, you were a full-on bitch sometimes."

"Well, okay," Lydia said.

"No, more like Bitchzilla," Nancy said with a laugh.

"Hey now!" Lydia said, laughing.

"Mega Bitchzilla Biotch!" Nancy said.

They were both laughing so hard that tears were streaming down their faces. They clutched at each other's hands, not wanting to let go.

Michael took a mental snapshot and tucked it away inside his head. He would keep this moment, the exact moment that the healing began.

Chapter Seventy-Three

Cassie reminded herself that it probably wouldn't be a good idea to hit Geoff in the face with a frying pan. What kind of example would that be for her baby?

They sat in silence. She knew that Dad and Chuck were in the kitchen, trying to give them space. Her dad had said something along the lines of, "It's about time you both had an adult conversation, since you want to be treated like adults." All they had done so far for fifteen minutes is catch each other staring and looking way. Over and over they played this game. Cassie knew that she wouldn't speak first, that it had to be Geoff to break the silence.

As she observed him, it was like she was seeing him for the first time. He seemed so young, just a boy really. She wondered what she had seen in him before. Yeah, he had great hair, a nice cleft in his chin and gorgeous blue eyes, but that was only surface stuff. She hadn't meant to get pregnant, but she had only envisioned the baby bringing them closer together. All it had done, in a round about way, was keep them apart.

She remembered how crushed she had been. Here she was, pregnant with this boy's baby. She had to tell him everything, all about who her Dad really was, who he had

292

been. Cassie couldn't have a baby with a guy and have secrets between them. She learned this from her Mom-Dad and her Dad-Dad. Watching them as they fell apart was so horrible. Her father had been broken when her dad had left them, when she had left to become he. When he had left to live the life that was meant to be his all along.

Eventually, they had gotten on with their lives, they had managed. They had grieved. But there was a rift between her father and her. Cassie had been a mommy's girl through and through. She missed her mother. Finding her again, even as he was now, was like finding a piece of herself.

She had laid all this out to Geoff. She had told him everything. She had known from about three minutes in, that it wasn't going to go well. Cassie knew at ten minutes in, that it was going horribly. She knew at fifteen minutes in, after she had finished speaking, that they were done.

She had grieved again. Grieved for what could have been. She would not be the first person to speak.

"I'm sorry," he said softly, his voice gruff with unsaid words.

"I know you are."

"What do we do?" He shook his head. "We're both too young for a baby. Way too young."

She sat silently for a moment before responding. "I have an idea," she said softly.

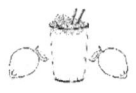

293

Poppy and Dava sat across from them on one of the couches. Cassie sat on the other one with Chuck and Sebastian on either side of her.

"I don't understand?" Poppy said this as if it was a question. She was clutching Dava's hand so tightly her knuckles had gone white.

"Well, I've talked it over with my Dad's and they think it's a good idea. I'm about four months pregnant. In five more months, I will have a baby." She paused again. "I'd like to give it to you."

"Why?" Poppy said. "Why would you do this?" She sounded dangerously close to tears.

Cassie took a moment before answering. "I know that you lost your baby. I'm having this baby and there's no way I could raise it. I have too much life left to live. I know it won't be the baby you were going to have, but I hope that it could be yours, nonetheless. She'll need someone to love her."

A tear broke free and slid down Poppy's cheek. "She?"

"I have a feeling it's a girl. It would make me so happy if you would take her, if you would make her yours."

Poppy and Dava were both crying now, the tears sliding down both their faces, but smiles had broken out. Poppy and Dava got up and hugged Cassie, squeezing her gently. There was such love and warmth in that room that Cassie knew she had never experienced anything like it.

"Thank you, thank you, thank you," Poppy said. She kissed both of Cassie's cheeks and hugged her again.

Behind Cassie, Chuck reached out to ruffle her hair. "I'm proud of you, kid."

"Yeah," Cassie said. "I'm proud of me too."

"That was a very mature decision you made," Sebastian put in.

A look of wonder crossed Cassie's face. "Shit. I'm fucking adulting!"

Chapter Seventy-Four

Rebecca was humming in the kitchen.

She was attempting to make lasagna. She had never made it before and wasn't really sure she knew what she was doing. She had the recipe book open on the counter and was following the instructions, but the problem was she was really good at *ordering* food. She just didn't know how to *make* it. *Oh well,* she thought. *It's pasta, meat, sauce and a fuckload of cheese. It should taste good no matter what I do.*

She had the table all set with a tablecloth and candles. She had put on some nice music. Enya was always soothing. She normally listened to her during yoga, but she was also good for dinner music, wasn't she? She looked at the table set with candle sticks and plates, silverware and glasses. She had put four places on the table. She went over to the table to make sure everything was still proper.

Rebecca was so happy. Devon was coming over with Curtis. They were finally going to have dinner all together like a family should. It would be the first time that Devon and Dillon had been in the same room in a long time, if you didn't count the night that she had met Dillon at the bar.

Doing a little twirl in the kitchen, Rebecca went about making garlic bread with more cheese and a Caesar salad to go with the lasagna. If she was going to go for it, she might as well go the whole way. Dillon came into the kitchen and put his arms around her while she was working at the counter.

"Smells good," Dillon said, nuzzling her neck.

"Thanks! I hope it doesn't kill anyone though."

"I don't think it will. If it does, we will all die together and there will be wine to wash it down."

"Ha, ha, ha. Your faith in me is astounding." She hit him on the butt with a spatula.

"I have immense faith in you." He looked uncomfortable for a second. "You'll have to add two more places at the table."

"Oh?" Rebecca turned to face him, a smile on her face. "Who's coming by?"

He took a moment to answer and looked even more uncomfortable. "Your mom and your aunt Jo."

The smile on Rebecca's face fell slightly. "Oh."

"I know I should have told you. I should have. Your mom called last night and said that she wanted to see you, and I thought how fortunate it was that we were having dinner with the boys and maybe if we had dinner with all of us together, it might take the stress of seeing your mom again for the first time in forever, and I'm so, so, so sorry." This was all said in one long breath.

"Oh," Rebecca said. "When will my mother be coming by?"

There was a knock at the door. "Um, now?" Dillon said. "I thought it would be better if they showed up before Devon and Curtis did."

"Oh," Rebecca said again.

"Please say something other than 'Oh'. I know you're pissed, but she's your mom. I think she loves you in her own way. Please, Babe."

"Okay," she said. "Okay. I can do this." There was another knock at the door. "You better go and let them in."

Rebecca slid the garlic bread into the oven and started tossing the salad. It would give her hands something to do rather than strangling her mother. Rebecca heard the door open and close and she heard Anna and Aunt Jo in the hallway. She started chopping the salad faster, almost savagely, as if the salad alone would pay for what her mother put her through.

Devon was talking and she could hear them speaking. Rebecca started chopping the salad even faster.

She heard footsteps behind her and there was sheer quiet in the kitchen before Rebecca heard a voice. "Hello Rebecca." It was her mother. Rebecca continued to make the salad and mixed the dressing into the leaves and cheese and squirted the lemon over everything. "Hello."

"Hello Rebecca darling!" Aunt Jo said.

Rebecca turned and cleaned off her hands so that she could envelope her aunt in a big hug. "Hello Auntie Jo! It's so wonderful to see you again."

Love and Lemonade

Her mother looked oddly hurt. Rebecca tried to be cheered by this but ended up feeling sad, so she held out her hand to Anna. "Hello Mother," Rebecca said. She tried to not sound like a bitch and could tell from the look on her mother's face that she wasn't entirely successful.

"Hello. How are you?" Anna asked, sounding stilted.

"I'm fine."

"Good. That's good."

"I need a fucking drink," Rebecca said. "Did you want a shot of something before we have wine with dinner?"

"God yes!" Anna said, coming over and smiling a genuine smile. "Do you have any sambuca?"

"Right here," Rebecca said, taking out a bottle from the cupboard above her head. "I always have a shot after fancier meals."

"Just like we used to do on holidays," Anna said. Her eyes were glassy with remembering. They stared at each other and something passed between them.

They poured out four shots of sambuca and they all drank. Things were easier after that. Alcohol had that effect on people. Dillon poured everyone some wine and they made their way to the living room so that they could be comfortable while Rebecca got everything else together. They boys had texted and said that they were only a few minutes away.

"Well, I do hope you enjoy dinner. Rebecca cooked everything," Dillon said.

"She did?" Aunt Jo asked. "The Rebecca I knew couldn't do more than boil an egg," she said with a grin.

"I'm not the Rebecca you knew," Rebecca said softly. There was a knock at the door and Rebecca went to get it this time.

Opening the door, she saw Devon who had his arm around a man that had to be Curtis. He was just what she had pictured when Devon had told her that he had met someone, oddly enough the same night that she had met Dillon.

"Curtis, its so nice to finally meet you," Rebecca said, stepping back to let them in the apartment. "Devon has told me a lot about you."

"Not all good, I hope?" Curtis said with a wink. "Just joking. I'm pretty awesome," he said. "It's lovely to meet you," Curtis said.

They walked in to find Jo and Anna sitting in the living room. The two women stood when Curtis and Devon entered. "Oh, please don't stand on my account," Curtis joked.

"Mom, Aunt Jo, this is Devon and his boyfriend Curtis."

"Charmed," Curtis said.

"Likewise," Jo said, pointing at Curtis. "You, sir, look like a spitfire. I love a man not afraid of a good time."

"Oh, gracious! Compliments before drinks? This is just too wonderful."

Dillon poured them both wine and they made their way to the table. He had added in the leaf and helped Rebecca to set the table again. Anna and Jo let out little sounds of amazement when they saw how lovely the table looked. When Rebecca brought the food to the table and the scents of her cooking filled the air, it put everyone at ease.

"I love a good lasagna," Curtis said. "I always used to ask for it for my birthday dinner, even though my birthday is in August. My mom made it though, despite the heat."

"Your mom sounds sweet," Rebecca said.

"She is. She never fails to call me every year at the exact time I was born…at one o'clock in the morning," he said with a grin.

The food was wonderful, and the conversation flowed easily. Throughout dinner, Dillon watched Rebecca and her mother. They didn't talk very much to each other, but they did talk. They were kind to each other, and Dillon knew that, while they had a long road ahead, they would all get there together.

Devon surprised them as Rebecca was about to serve dessert. Rebecca was serving fresh berries with homemade whipped cream and honey. "Nancy called earlier this morning. He wants us all to come to Blaine's exhibition of paintings at the art gallery."

"Blaine is having an exhibition? I knew he painted…," Rebecca said.

"Yeah, he's really nervous. The more people there, the better Nancy said."

"Well I love art," Anna said. "I hope you have a lovely time." She looked disappointed to be calling the evening an end.

"Don't be silly mom," Rebecca said. "You should come with us. Nancy did say the more people the better."

"Oh, we couldn't impose," Anna said.

"Please," Rebecca said. She reached out and clasped her mother's free hand. "I'd love it if you both came."

"Oh!" She drew in a shaky breath. "We'd be delighted then."

There was a silence afterwards, but it felt warm and full of promise. Dillon sat there, watching the woman that he wanted to make his wife. He looked down at his pocket quickly and pictured the diamond ring inside of the black velvet box.

He could only hope that she would say yes.

Chapter Seventy-Five

Joe helped Cordellia with the clasp of the diamond necklace around her neck.

"I'm surprised that you're wearing this tonight," he said.

"Why? It's not every day that my son has his own art show. His own art exhibition, Joe! I never thought I would see the day. Can you believe it?"

"I can," Joe said. "Blaine was always talented. You must be very proud."

"I am. Which is why I don't understand about the necklace."

"You told me that you threw out everything Romilda gave you when you were together."

"And so I did," she said. "Everything but this," she said.

"Why? Why did you hold onto that?"

"Because it was the night that she left to have his operation. The night that she told me to go to you."

Joe looked shocked. He stood there with his coat in one hand and his shirt only half tucked in. "What do you mean?"

"Exactly that. Blaine had just been born. Edward... Romilda was going to Montreal to have her operation. He gave me this necklace that night. At first I thought it was his way of an apology." She fingered the silver and diamond necklace lovingly. "She couldn't be who she wasn't anymore. I asked her why give me the necklace then, why bother spending such an extreme amount of money on me when I was probably going to throw it away. She said it was for you. So I could look beautiful for you."

"Romilda said that?" Joe's voice was a whisper.

"Yes. She knew that I was miserable, that I had come back to him out of obligation. Now that she was going away, she told me to find you, to go back to you, to make a life with you instead of a lie with him," she said. "Told me she wanted me to shine so brightly that you could find me even in the darkness."

"I see. That was very brave."

"It was. I never thought of them when I wore this necklace. I always associated it with you. I wore it at night when I was lonely or I would let the necklace run through my fingers, imagining it was your fingers laced through mine."

"I love you so much, Cordellia," he said gruffly.

"I love you too, so very much. That's why your plan isn't going to work."

"What plan?"

"What plan do you think?

Joe sighed and tucked in his shirt. While he was putting on his coat, he said, "I've decided, Cordy. It's my decision. I don't want to put you through any of that. None of that. I don't want you to watch me waste away. I can't put you through that."

"No," she said.

"No?"

"No, you don't get to decide that for me. I don't remember you discussing the option of assisted suicide. We never had that discussion, did we? So I choose no."

"Cordellia…"

"No, you listen to me. I spent thirty years waiting for you, pining for you, wishing for you. Every breath I took into my body wished for you and every breath I let out was really saying your name."

Tears were sliding down her face. "You don't get to decide this for me. What did the doctors say? Really? Tell me, how long do you have?"

"They say it's anywhere from four months to a year. They don't know how long I have. I could go tomorrow, I could go next week, or a month from now. They weren't sure."

"Good then, neither are you," Cordellia said.

"Cordellia, I have stage four prostate cancer."

"So, I have small tits."

"Cordellia, listen!"

"No, you listen Joe! I have waited too long for you, too long picturing your face in my dreams, hoping for your touch along my skin. You were selfish to want to take yourself away from me, so now I'm going to be selfish and keep you with me until your last breath. Do you hear me?"

"Cordellia…" He didn't know what to say.

"No, Joe. When we got married, didn't we promise to love each other? So let me love you, let me love all of you. I will take care of you and if need be fill you with so many drugs that you wouldn't feel a thing. I know a very good pot dealer. Could you imagine? We could hold a pot party! Wouldn't that be something?" she said with a wistful twinkle in her eyes.

Joe sighed. "You're not going to give up on this, are you?"

"No, I won't. I'm afraid your stuck with me. Now let's go, we're going to be late for Blaine's opening." She kissed him. "Also, your fly is down." She gave him a wicked grin.

Chapter Seventy-Six

"So, which one of you fuckers is going to pay for the beer?" Blaine said.

Nancy, the delightful one, fruity if you will, shrugged. "I can't. I just got one of your paintings and haven't gotten any of my author royalties yet." He shrugged. "I'm fresh out."

He looked at Chuck, who was always up for a good time. "Sorry man, I have a family to think about," he said, putting an arm around Sebastian and Cassie. "Besides, why are you paying for booze at your own art show? That's fucked up."

"Oh," Blaine said. "Right."

"Blaine, you need to drink more. You're a little out of it," Mike said.

"He was always out of it," William said. "Remember the time that we were in the bathroom in The Cabin and couldn't find a toilet?"

"I don't recall that particular episode of debauchery," Blaine said.

"I'd like to hear about said episode of debauchery," Justin said. "There's so much I don't know."

"Don't pester the boy," Victoria said. "Here honey, have some more booze. What do you call this? It's lovely."

"It's a drink of my own making," Cordellia said. "It's pink lemonade and vodka with a bit of lime juice thrown in for a bit of taste."

"I would have made it with tequila," Victoria said. "But that's just me."

"Hmm," Poppy said. "I always loved champagne and pink lemonade. Remember the time we did that one New Years Eve?"

"We'll have to suggest that to Kaitlin at the Whip," Dava said. "She's always looking for drink suggestions."

"I don't know, I'd rather pink lemonade and gin," William said. "Zack made some of those last night. Tart and you can't taste the gin. Goes down faster that way."

"Well, you like some things fast, but others slow," Zack joked.

"Ugh, there are children present," Cassie said.

"You are hardly a child. But you're my child, so I'll let that stand," Sebastian said.

All around Blaine there was the sound of people as they strolled around looking at the paintings that he had created. Thirty large canvasses plus ten smaller ones interspersed throughout the whole gallery. Forty works in all, each of a person that he knew or had known, or someone who had touched his life.

Much like everyone in the room, he saw Romilda walking with Gaston, spotted Connie walking arm in arm with a woman. Devon and Curtis were walking around with

Rebecca and her mother and aunt, Anna and Jo. He saw Mo Seagrave walking arm in arm with a man that must be her partner. There were more people than even he knew. He must have seen a few hundred walk through the gallery, perhaps more than that. All around him there was conversation and laughter and people looking at what he had created.

"Pretty amazing isn't it?" Cordellia said from beside him.

"A little mind blowing, actually."

"I think it's amazing," Cordellia said. "I'm so proud of you, Blaine. I always told you that you would amount to something grand."

"And as usual, you were right," Blaine said with a soft smile.

Cordellia smiled and squeezed his hand.

He watched Remy place a red sticker on another of the cards below a canvass. She turned and saw him and smiled brightly as she walked toward him. "I'd say this evening has been a rousing success!"

"I'd say so!" Blaine said. "I'm happy that so many people have come. I know I sold a few paintings, so that's good, too."

Remy calked her head to the right. "A few? Blaine, haven't you looked at all the red stickers?"

"I've been too afraid to, actually," he said, blushing.

"Well, you've sold every single one."

Blaine found that he couldn't find his voice. "Every one?" he choked out.

"Every single one and all the art cards as well."

"There were over one hundred sets of those," Justin said.

"Yes, isn't it marvellous? People are already asking when you're going to have your next art show. I've started taking down names and numbers. We should probably get you a web site and some business cards, huh?"

Remy gave Blaine a hug. "Congratulations. I want you to go out tonight and celebrate. At the price we've been selling your paintings at, you are gong to be a very happy man."

She walked away, each click of her high heel shoes on the hardwood floor sounding to Blaine like some kind of music. Everyone around Blaine was looking at him with wide smiles on their faces. Justin pulled him in for a kiss.

"Blaine, are you okay?" he asked.

"I don't know yet. I'll let you know when I stop floating!"

"I know just what we need!" Cordellia said. "I'll go get more pink lemonade!"

Epilogue

Four Months later, February 14th

Cordellia knew that Joe was nervous.

She could feel him vibrating beside her. Though he was sitting still, she would feel his movement from the inside, as if his whole being was shaking.

"This is a shitty Valentine's Day, I'm sorry darlin'. I wanted to take you somewhere special and do something wonderful," Joe said.

"How many times do I have to tell you? Anything I do with you is wonderful. Having coffee, going shopping. Even taking out the garbage."

"But you make me take out the garbage."

"I know!" Cordellia said. "That's why it's wonderful." She gave him a soft smile and a kiss on the cheek.

A nurse came out to them. "Joe? The doctor is ready to see you." She gave him a wide smile. "Come on, I'll bring you through.

She led them to the doctor's office and opened the door. Dr. Carlisle stood up and held out her hand to shake Joe's, then Cordellia's. "I'm so happy to see you both today." She closed the door. "I have news. We got back the results of your last CT scans."

"Well, lay it on me doctor. How much time do I have left?" Joe said. His face was set in grim lines and he squeezed Cordellia's hand. He took strength from her touch.

"Well, that's just it." Doctor Carlisle took out his folder and opened it to show him. "You have all the time in the world."

Cordellia shook her head. "I'm afraid I don't understand. What is it your saying?"

"Well, we don't have any explanation for this, but it has been known to happen in rare cases. It appears that this is one of them."

"What is this chart telling me?" Joe asked.

"Your cancer is in remission," Doctor Carlisle said. "It seems you've been given a reprieve, Joe." She smiled and it was a truly bright smile. "Now, you'll still have to come to the hospital every so often so we can run test for the first year to make sure that you stay in remission, but for now, keep doing what you're doing."

"I-I don't understand," Joe said. "What are you saying? That I'm okay? I'm not going to die?"

"Not today, not tomorrow, maybe not for long time. Everything will have to be watched, but yes, for now you are not going to die."

"What do you think did it?" Cordellia asked.

"I know what did it," Joe said. "Being loved by you. You wouldn't let me quit, even when I wanted to. Even when I wanted to let go."

"Well, they do say that love is the greatest medicine there is," Doctor Carlisle said. "I want you to do me a favour."

"Anything," Joe said.

"Go out and celebrate tonight."

"I will! Tonight, and every night."

When they were outside the doctor's office, Joe pulled Cordellia in for a deep kiss. When the kiss broke, he looked at her, life restored in his eyes. "I love you Cordellia."

"And I love you, Joe, so much."

"Do you think it's too early for some vodka and pink lemonade?" he asked.

She shrugged. "Hey, it's beer o'clock somewhere in the world!"

End of Love and Lemonade

The Lemonade Series Book Three

Jamieson Wolf

Acknowledgements

There are a few people I'd like to thank for helping me during the writing of this novel.

Michael, you continue to amaze me. Not only did you help with the titles of each of the book in the Lemonade Series, you listened to me as I wondered aloud about what would happen to them and gave me sage advice that helped to make the novels better. You are not only my husband but also my lover and best friend. My life would not sparkle without you.

To my family: thank you. Thank you for giving me the support and the encouragement that I needed to continue writing when I felt like giving up. Thanks go out to my Wonder Mom Susan and my Wonder Dad Chris. Also, to my Wonder Mother in Law Helen and to Bev. You've all been such a great cheering section; you make the act of writing easier to do.

Thanks go out to my family of the heart as well. You are the people who make my spirit happy, who fill me up with sparkles when I am low and who fill me with so much joy. It is an honour to have you as part of my heart family. Thanks go out to Meaghan, Karine, Christine, Alexandra, Remington, Rachael, Stephanie, Jackie, Dava and Kimberlee.

Lastly, thanks go out to Nathan Caro Frechette and everyone at Renaissance Press. Thank you for giving Blaine and company a home and for helping them to grow. Without all of you, the characters in these novels would remained solely inside of my head. You gave them space to stretch out and play.

To all of you, I give thanks.

About the author

Jamieson has been writing since a young age when he realized he could be writing instead of paying attention in school. Since then, he has created many worlds in which to live his fantasies and live out his dreams.

He is a number-one bestselling author—he likes to tell people that a lot—and writes in many different genres. He is the author of over sixty books. Jamieson is also an accomplished artist and he works with acrylic paint. He is also an amateur photographer.

He currently lives in Ottawa Ontario Canada with his husband Michael. You can contact Jamieson through this website at www.jamiesonwolf.com

Renaissance.
Diverse Canadian Voices

Renaissance was founded in May 2013 by a group of friends who wanted to publish and market those stories which don't always fit neatly in a genre, or a niche, or a demographic.

This is still the type of story we are drawn to; however, we've also noticed another interesting trend in what we tend to publish. It turns out that we are naturally drawn to the voices of those who are members of a marginalized group (especially people with disabilities and LGBTQIAPP2+ people), and these are the voices we want to continue to uplift. Our team is the same; we seem to naturally surround ourselves with people who are, like us, people with marginalized identities.

To us, Renaissance isn't just a business; it's a found family. Being authors and artists ourselves, we care as much about our authors enjoying the publishing process as we do about our readers enjoying a great story and seeing a new perspective.

pressesrenaissancepress.ca
pressesrenaissancepress@gmail.com

978-1-987963-62-5

The Lemonade series

by Jamieson Wolf

In a world filled with one-night stands, glory hole blowjobs and weeklong romances, what does it take to find love? This is just what our protagonist Blaine worries about. Unlike his friends, he wants to settle down.

Vol 1:   978-1-987963-24-3

Vol 2:   978-1-987963-36-6

978-1-987963-47-2

THE STEALTH LOVERS
by Cait Gordon

After submitting to mandatory conscription, two young men begin Basic Training, or, "Vacay in Hay."

Xaxall Dwyer Knightly saunters onto base without a care in the worlds, filled to the brim with sass. He has the strength of five warriors and earns the distinction of being the only trainee to throw someone through a supporting wall.

Vivoxx Nathan Tirowen, son of a prominent general, carries himself with a naturally-commanding presence. Possessing an uncanny talent with weaponry, his drill sergeant is convinced Vivoxx could "trim the pits of a rodent without nicking the skin."

When the two recruits meet, one smiles warmly while the other speaks gibberish. Little do they know the bond they feel will lead them to become the venerable military pairing known as

The Stealth.

"The fiercest, most formidable warrior-lovers in the 'Cosm are back. And the battle has never been so fabulous!"
—Stephen Graham King, author of A Congress of Ships

"Cait Gordon sent us on a ride full of pew-pew physics and one of the absolute best traits of people: our humour."
—'Nathan Burgoine, Lambda Literary finalist and author of Light

"HOLY STARS, I loved everything about this novel!!!"
—Jamieson Wolf, author of Little Yellow Magnet

Run J Run

by Su J Sokol

Jeremy, a high school English teacher coming to grips with a shattered marriage and haunted by the brother he lost, unexpectedly falls in love with his best friend, Zak. Attractive, wildly unconventional, and happy in an open relationship with his partner Annie, Zak seems to embody everything missing from Jeremy's life, but when the arrest and death of a marginalized student at the Brooklyn high school where they both teach trigger Zak's mental breakdown and slow descent, Jeremy and Annie are compelled to cross boundaries, both external and internal, in a desperate attempt to save him.

"This gripping story takes us into the deepest recesses of trauma and makes us look at family and therapy in unconventional but convincing ways." H. Nigel Thomas, author of *No Safeguards*, finalist for the Paragraphe Hugh MacLennan Prize for fiction

"Run J Run is a compelling chronicle of a tumultuous, erotically charged friendship imperilled by madness." David Demchuk, author of *The Bone Mother*, nominee for the Giller Prize and winner of the Sunburst Award for Excellence in Canadian Fiction of the Fantastic

"There are living breathing people here." Barry Webster, author of The Lava in My Bones, finalist for the Lambda Literary Award

"Run J Run is a sophisticated depiction of sexual awakening and mental illness. Marvellous, compelling and vital." Arshad Kahn, filmmaker

978-1-987963-51-9

Murder at the World's Fair

By MJ Lyons

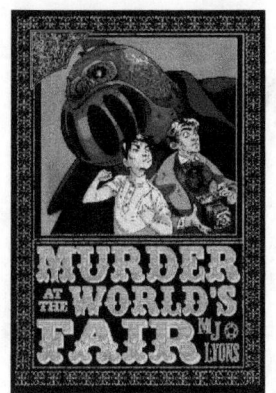

The year is 1893, and airships cloud the skies over the bustling metropolis of Toronto, set to host the world's fair.

On the day of the grand opening, young Norwood Quigley, aspiring journalist, photographer and scion of a world-famous airship magnate, stumbles onto the scene of a murder; the victim: a Prussian Ambassador; the perpetrator: a Chinese assassin, or so the powers-that-be say. In truth, the suspect is Jing, a roguish but amiable youthful delinquent.

Concerned by Jing's claim of innocence, Norwood is thrown into a grand intrigue that hinges on Toronto's world fair.

"A nimble, inventive steampunk romp — complete with clockwork cats, daring escapes, beguiling romance and shadowy mysteries —that you'll rip through in one sitting and beg for the next."
—Matthew Bright, author of The Library of Lost Things

"Alternate reality? Set at the turn of the 19th century? During a World's Fair? With a murder mystery; clockwork monsters; a wonderfully genuine and familiar family dynamic; and romance? Pair all that with beautiful and evocative writing, and you've got a stunning debut.."
—KD Edwards, author of the *The Last Sun* and *The Hanged Man*

978-1-987963-54-0

A CONGRESS OF SHIPS

BY STEPHEN GRAHAM KING

In a desolate system on the outer edge of Pan Galactum, the skin of the universe has ruptured, tearing open a portal to an alternate reality. Witnessed only by the sentient science vessel N'Dea, a massive, battered ship falls through, housing a community of refugees fleeing an enemy that has pursued them across the cold reaches of space for decades.

But have they come alone?

Summoned by N'Dea while en route from a reunion with dear friends on the Galactum's capital, the mystery is a lure that fellow Artificial Sentience, the Maverick Heart, cannot resist. It's now up to Vrick, along with humans Keene, Lexa-Blue and Ember, and allies old and new, to come to the aid of this ship of lost souls. Together they must find a way to seal the breach for good, before a ravening hunger can spill through and rip the Galactum apart.

"Stephen Graham King's Maverick Heart Cycle is the queer Firefly-meets-Killjoys series I always wanted, with the added bonus of his seemingly effortless world-building, clever plots, and themes of chosen family and "no one left behind" that bring me back every time. Trust me: go get squishy." —Nathan Burgoine, author of *Light* **and** *Exit Plans for Teenage Freaks*

"The entire series is a must-read." —Cait Gordon, author of *Life in the 'Cosm* **and** *The Stealth Lovers*.